SHUTOUT

A Seattle Sockeyes Puck Brothers Novel

JAMI DAVENPORT

The Scoring Series #1

Cover by Kim Killion of The Killion Group.

Cover Image by Wander Aguiar

The Seattle Sockeyes®, Seattle Steelheads®, and Seattle Skookums™ are fictional sports teams. Game On in Seattle™ is a series of sports romance novels The names and logos are created for the sole use of the owner and covered under protection of trademark.

Jami Davenport®, Seattle Sockeyes®, and Seattle Steelheads® are registered trademarks with the United States Patent and Trademark Office.

This book is a work of fiction. While references might be made to actual historical events or existing locations, the names, characters, places, and incidents are either the product of the author's imagination or are used fictitiously, and any resemblance to actual persons, living or dead, business establishments, events, or locales is entirely coincidental.

Warning

This book contains sexually explicit scenes and adult language and may be considered offensive to some readers. This book is for sale to adults ONLY, as defined by the laws of the country in which you made your purchase. Please store your files wisely, where they cannot be accessed by under-age readers.

Email: jamidavenport@hotmail.com

Website: https://www.jamidavenport.com

Twitter: @jamidavenport

Facebook: https://www.facebook.com/jamidavenport

Author Page: https://www.facebook.com/jamidavenportauthor

Sign up for Jami's Newsletter: https://eepurl.com/LpfaL

❀ Created with Vellum

BLURB

Easton:

Hockey isn't forever.

The money, excitement, and glory of being a professional hockey player meant more to me than a family, a home, and a forever. Another man has my forever, and I have hockey. I thought making the big bucks and playing against the best in the world would feel better than this. Instead I'm empty and hollow, like a big piece of my heart was hacked off. There's something missing. Something big. Something I can never get back.

Caroline:

I loved him, but he wasn't the love of my life.

My husband died too young, too suddenly, too tragically. I was unprepared with no education, no job skills, and no future plans. When a DNA test reveals my twins' true parentage, I have no choice but to do the right thing. I turn to the one man who'd turned his back on me all those years ago.

I'd been shut out from his life, and I'd shut him out from mine. Can two strangers make a family? Do we have what it takes to forgive and move on?

To Tera, my fabulous editor, who always does her best to make my books better.

While starting a new series is exhilarating and motivating, it's also daunting and scary. An author never truly knows how a series will be received by their readers. All we can do is write the best book we can and hope and pray it hits the mark.

"The Scoring Series" is a continuation of the Seattle Sockeyes®. *Shutout* takes place the season following the team's championship season. These are the young guys on the team, many of them rookies. I hope you'll follow their stories as they fight to score in professional hockey, life, and love.

Thank you for following me on this journey. It's been an incredible ride so far, and I hope we'll be together for many years to come.

PROLOGUE

Two Years Prior

--Easton--

*B*eing a stalker was new to me, but I was a quick learner.

I wasn't able to find her on social media. Either she didn't have a profile or she'd locked it down, which wouldn't be unusual for a cautious single woman who always thought stuff through rather than flying by the seat of her pants like I had the tendency to do.

Once I'd made my decision, I'd tracked Caroline down via an online service and paid forty dollars to get her address.

I hadn't seen her in years.

I'd never been a huge hookup guy. More of a guy who dated a woman exclusively. I'd been dating the same woman all through my first few years of college, and we'd recently broken up. The split had been mutual. The relationship had run its course. I found myself looking for something I'd lost, something I'd walked away from, and wondering what could have been.

I guess I was feeling melancholy.

Hockey had always been enough for me, but lately it wasn't. I was searching for that elusive thing called happiness, and eventually I turned to Caroline.

Chalk it all up to loneliness.

Caroline and I had enjoyed each other for a couple months when we were both teens. I'd been in Chicago for a summer hockey program taught by a well-known, highly respected former professional player. She'd just finished high school one year early and was working at the rink where I was skating.

I'd ended it and most likely broken her heart. I hadn't given her much thought until lately. Oh, there'd been moments when she'd invaded my sleep or crept into my daydreams. We were both older, hopefully wiser, and I was curious what'd happened to her.

So here I was. Prepared to see if the old spark might still be there.

I parked my rental car with the heavily tinted windows across the street from her address and waited, praying her neighbors wouldn't notice and call the police. She lived in a nice subdivision near Chicago comprised of newer homes. The kind of subdivision families lived in, not normally a place where singles lived. I ignored that red flag. She probably rented a room with a few other women, or maybe she was a nanny. The Caro I knew had ambitions. She was going places. Her life was completely mapped out, while I'd just stumbled through life with only one goal in mind—playing professional hockey.

Hours later, I'd consumed most of my sandwich and soda with no sign of Caro. I was ready to give up when the front door opened. An average-sized guy walked out holding the hand of a little girl with blonde curls. I wasn't good at judging kids' ages, but she couldn't be more than a few years old.

This had to be the wrong address.

I was about to turn the key in the ignition when the door opened again. A beautiful blonde woman hurried out the door, chasing a little boy, who barreled toward the man. The man picked him up and spun him around, while the woman smiled up at them. I heard their laughter through my rolled-up windows.

Pain slammed into me harder than a sucker punch by the best enforcer in the league. Agony burned through my veins to every part of my body until the anguish was so great I went numb. I didn't know how my lungs continued to breathe in the air around me or how my heart managed to keep pumping. Surely, it'd formed multiple cracks in the last several seconds.

My strong reaction caught me off guard. Yeah, what we'd had had been fucking hot, and I'd like a do-over on ending it, but to have it affect me like this? I shook off the unwelcome emotions and denied their existence. Ours had been a young love, nothing more.

I stared, willing my mind to make sense of what I was seeing, to tell me this wasn't her but an apparition. No matter how hard I tried to convince myself this woman wasn't Caroline Jones, I knew the truth. I knew her smile, her laugh, the way the sun glinted off her golden hair, the way she tilted her head when she was listening intently. I knew the way her body moved with the grace of a gazelle. Yeah, I knew it all.

And there was one more thing I knew.

This guy had Caro and his kids, while I had hockey.

I'm not sure which one of us was luckier.

Chapter One

NEW BEGINNINGS

--Caroline--

*H*e might not have been the love of my life, but I loved him.

And now he was gone.

Mark was buried in a hole, and I was left to raise six-year-old twins on my own.

That fatal night over three months ago seemed like yesterday. The knock on the door, the policeman standing on my porch at one a.m., the panic rising inside me at the grim look on his face. Mark had been late getting home from work. Nothing unusual there. My husband had been a workaholic. He'd apparently fallen asleep at the wheel and perished in a fiery crash. He'd only been a mile from home.

Ours had been a comfortable relationship, not a white-hot passion, not even in the beginning. He'd been a good provider, a great father, and a decent man. He'd treated me well. I had no complaints.

For three months, I'd struggled with my new reality. Now it was September. My six-year-old twins were in first grade, and I was a twenty-four-year-old single mother without a career. I needed to fight past my grief and devise a plan for my future and my children's. It was time.

I'd struggled my entire life with a niggling doubt I'd never be good enough. I'd depended on Mark and his family to take care of me, while I'd done nothing to take care of myself or have personal security if the worst should happen. And the worst had happened.

I was the daughter of an alcoholic father who couldn't hold down a job and a mother who went through men as quickly as she changed outfits. I'd been told my entire childhood that I was worthless and screwed up everything I touched. The summer after I'd graduated high school and gotten a full-ride academic scholarship, I'd found out I was pregnant and proven them right again.

For the next six-plus years, I'd concentrated on being the best wife and mother possible, and I'd pulled it off. Without Mark to depend on, those insecurities came flooding back.

Mark had a small life insurance policy, which covered our living expenses for about a year. The clock was ticking, and I'd wasted three months already. I needed a career plan, and I needed it yesterday.

Not knowing what else to do, I drove to my in-laws' house. They'd become the parents I'd never had. Howard Mills had recently retired with intentions to move to a warmer Arizona. The only things holding them back were the kids and me.

Fran opened the door before I knocked and wrapped me in her arms for a warm hug. I hugged her back and squeezed my eyes shut to stem the tears that were so close to the surface every time I saw Mark's parents.

Fran stood back and ushered me into her inviting house. Soon I was seated on the patio in the afternoon sun with a glass of wine in my hand.

"Where's Howard?" I asked.

"Golfing. Where else?" Fran smiled kindly at me. These people had been my rock since Mark had died. They'd been there for me at every turn, and guilt rose inside me with the knowledge they were postponing their retirement plans because I was an emotional mess wandering without direction.

"Of course." I took a sip, savoring the simple pleasure of a good bottle of wine.

We chatted about nothing for several minutes. She told me about their search for an Arizona house. Throughout our conversation, the underlying current of sadness floated below the surface. Fran, who'd always been proud of her appearance, had aged at least ten years since Mark had died, as had Howard. My heart bled for them, just as it bled for my children. We were all struggling to deal with our grief in the best way possible.

"How are the kids doing?" She'd seen them a few days ago, so she was well aware, but always hopeful, she lived for the day I'd say they were doing well.

"Not much has changed. Heath is noncommunicative and sullen except when he's playing hockey. Hailey is the opposite, acting out and demanding attention."

"I'm so sorry they're going through this. If I could take on their pain, I would."

"I know. We all would. Only time will heal the wounds for all of us." If I had a dollar for each time I'd said those very words in the past three months, I'd be a wealthy woman.

"Mark's life may have ended, but ours continue on," she said.

"Fran," I said, saying the one thing that'd been on my mind for the past month. "I don't want to hold you guys back. Don't stay here on my account."

"You're family, the only family we have left. We're here for you because we want to be. Your happiness and the twins' are our number one priority."

I so wanted to be worthy of their devotion, but I also had to stand on my own two feet and find my way in this world. "I appreciate your concern. You know I do. I can't let the two of you continue to sacrifice for me. I'm a big girl. Mark's life insurance will cover expenses for a while until I get things on track."

"I wish Mark had left more or that there was something we could do."

"You gave birth to and raised an outstanding man who cared for us, made sure we didn't lack for anything, and kept us safe. You've done more than most parents."

Fran's stricken expression caught me off guard. I searched my statement for something that might be upsetting to her and came up with nothing but confusion.

"Fran? What's wrong? What did I say?"

Fran stared at the hands clenched tightly in her lap. When she met my gaze, her expression was guilt-ridden. "I never gave birth to Mark."

"What?" Her voice had been so low I'd barely heard what she said and had obviously misinterpreted her words.

"There's something you should know, something we never told Mark, and I live with that mistake every day."

I frowned, and my stomach clenched as my imaginative brain ran through the possibilities. "What is it?"

"Don't look so stricken. It's not bad, just something you should know. Mark should've known, too, be we never found a way to stop perpetuating the lie."

"What lie?"

"We aren't his birth parents."

"You aren't?" My mouth fell open, and I gaped at her in absolute surprise. "But he looks so much like you and Howard."

"That made our secret so much easier to keep. We adopted him as a newborn. His real mother never saw his face, never got to hold him. We understand she was very young, and the father wasn't in the picture."

"I had no idea."

"Nor did Mark." Fran's face was lined with guilt. "We denied Mark the right to know his family. I don't want that to happen to the twins. They have a right to a relationship with people who share their genetics."

"No matter what, you'll always be their grandparents, genetics be damned."

Fran's eyes were unusually misty, and she dabbed at them with a napkin. "As a nurse, I'm fully aware genetics play an important part in a person's health."

I nodded, not sure what she was getting at exactly. Being a worrier,

I immediately jumped to the worst conclusion. Had Mark had some kind of hereditary health issue I wasn't aware of?

"Don't panic, Caro." Fran reached out and patted my hand, guessing accurately what I'd been thinking. "There's one half of the twins' relatives we know nothing about. I'd been meaning to have this conversation with Mark, but I'd put it off until too late. Now I can only fix it for his children. I think you need to have them DNA tested. I've looked into it, and via DNA testing on a popular genealogy site, you'll be able to find out close matches for relatives, background, and possible genetic health concerns."

"I don't know," I hedged, not sure why I was balking at this idea.

"Heath and Hailey most likely have another set of grandparents, aunts, uncles, cousins... They deserve to know them, especially considering we have such a small family unit. Why not expand that unit?"

"What if they're not interested in knowing them?"

"Then that will be that. No harm done. Wouldn't you rather know than not know? What if Mark has parents out there who wonder about him? Howard and I always thought there'd be time to tell Mark he was adopted. We waited for the right moment, and we waited too long. I don't want to make such a mistake with his children. They deserve to know, and we need to know."

Fran needed to know. I understood her guilt and her dilemma. Out there somewhere was a family we knew nothing about with their own life stories. I recalled filling out a form for my health insurance that asked several questions about the health of my relatives and known health issues in my family. My twins would be at a disadvantage as they'd only have one half of the picture. The more I thought about it, the more curious I was about these mystery people who shared a portion of my children's DNA. Genetics played a larger role in our lives than many of us cared to admit.

"Okay, what could it hurt? How do we do this?"

"I took the liberty of sending for kits. They're on the desk." She smiled gratefully at me, and the guilt lines on her face softened. "Mark would want this."

I nodded agreement. I didn't know what Mark would want, but he wasn't here to tell us.

Chapter Two

THE PUCK BROTHERS

--Easton--

*W*e were the young guys.

The guys with our entire NHL careers ahead of us.

We were cocky. We had the world by the tail, and nothing and no one could stop us. Our mutual love of partying and women had brought us together, along with our complete and total disinterest in long-term relationships. It was safe to say that every one of us had been burned before and learned our lessons. I knew I had. I might've been a one-woman man before, but now I played the field, didn't stay with one woman more than a week, and didn't get attached.

We were also wasted drunk and worried as hell about who would make the final cuts tomorrow, but none of us expressed our doubts. After all, we were invincible.

The regular season started the first week of October. We'd battled for a spot through the last two weeks of preseason games in September. Now it was showtime.

Axel raised his glass and grinned at us. Half of his beer sloshed over the side and soaked our nachos. We didn't care. We raised our glasses for our tenth toast of the night.

"To the"—Axel paused, deep in thought, mostly because his inebriated brain was soggy with alcohol—"the Puck Brothers! Long may we puck and fuck and have lots of luck."

"Hear! Hear!" we said in unison.

"The Puck Brothers. I like that." Ziggy burped and bumped fists with Axel. "And as the first official meeting of the Puck Brothers"—Ziggy held up his right hand, and the rest of us followed his lead—"we'll hit our pucks in the net, keep our dicks well exercised, and live life to the fullest."

"Hear! Hear!" I slurred.

Steele, who rarely said much, raised a hand like he was in fucking grade school. All heads turned to him, because raising his hand was just plain weird, even to our alcohol-muddled brains.

"What?" Axel, our self-appointed leader, asked over the rim of his beer glass.

"We might not all make the team."

Axel frowned and narrowed his eyes. "We're making the team. All of us. We're inseparable." His gaze swiveled to two women walking by in tight dresses so short a guy could see the bottoms of their delectable asses.

Steele blinked a few times, as if confused, and shook his head. "If you say so."

"I say so." Axel's eyes stayed glued to the blonde's ass.

"Skate and party till we drop. We'll play the field and enjoy every minute of it. We are the Puck Brothers," Kaden shouted and raised his glass. Answering shouts of agreement and clinking glasses solidified our Puck Brotherhood.

"Let's sweeten the pot. First one to bite it, we're gonna take it out on their ass."

More drunken shouts of agreement, even though most of us had zero idea what we were agreeing to.

Steele raised his hand again. "Bite what—monogamy?"

We all stared at each other and roared with laughter. Was this guy for real?

"Yup," Ziggy said.

"How will we determine if someone has bitten it? And who chooses the penalty?"

More eye-rolling and groans and snickering.

"Don't know. We'll decide when we need to."

"But—" Steele still took issue with our lack of clear rules.

Kaden emptied the last of the pitcher into his glass and took a long swallow before answering, "Whatever. We don't need rules. We're having fun here."

"Hear! Hear!" Axel raised his glass, and we did another toast. Steele didn't ask any more dumb-assed questions, so I guess he was mollified.

We toasted one more time. I guzzled the last of my beer and looked to the future. Life was fucking good.

Chapter Three

A WORLD TURNED UPSIDE DOWN

--Caroline--

The first week of October, Fran called me over to her house. The results had arrived.

When I got there, Fran was pacing back and forth in front of the desk in the den, and Howard was seated in front of the monitor. The screen was dark. He had the patience of a saint and was solid as a rock.

He winked at me and indicated one of the chairs placed in a semi-circle in front of the monitor. "Are you ready for this?"

I nodded and slumped into my seat. Fran sat next to me, fidgeting. I clasped my hands in my lap so tightly my fingernails dug into my palms, but the pain didn't distract me. I was edgy and nervous for reasons I couldn't explain. I didn't know Mark's biological relatives, and there was nothing to worry about, but worrying was my middle name.

"Did you peek?" I asked them.

Howard gave me one of those looks that said, *I can't believe you're asking me this*. Fran shook her head.

"He wouldn't let me," Fran said.

"All right then." Howard woke up the computer and navigated to the home page of the genealogy app. He logged in. "I took the liberty of reading through their instructions. Let's jump right to the meat of the matter. We'll review the closest DNA matches to see what we can find. Everyone ready?"

I chewed on my lower lip, and Fran gripped the arms of her chair. We both nodded.

Whatever was inside had the possibility of profoundly affecting my twins' lives, and I hoped we were doing the right thing. As my grandmother used to say, sometimes it was best to let sleeping dogs lie. What if we awoke not just a dog but a monster? What if my twins' grandfather was a criminal? Or even worse, a serial killer? My imagination took hold and threatened to run wild. I forcibly tamped it down.

"Let's do this," I said with more confidence than I felt.

Howard clicked on the menu option for viewing possible DNA matches. We held our collective breaths, and even Howard's hand shook ever so slightly. The list was somewhat long and arranged by highest level of DNA shared to lowest.

The first name on the list hit me like a punch to the gut. I blinked several times as the screen swam in front of me. I stared hard at the top name, certain I was hallucinating or having a bad dream or needed to be locked up in the psych ward. All those options were preferable to the truth screaming through every brain cell in my skull. The room was so hot, so very hot. I was being smothered by the heat.

I'd expected to see a list of names I didn't recognize. That wasn't the case.

The room spun around me. I tried to focus, but I was looking down a long tunnel of blurry images from my past. My spine turned to mush, refusing to hold up my body. I leaned to one side, leaned more, and more. The chair tipped, and I fell into a black abyss of blissful nothingness.

I woke on the couch with Fran sitting beside me and Howard hovering in the background. Pillows elevated my feet.

"What happened?" I heard a shaky voice ask the question and looked around for the speaker before realizing that'd been my voice.

"You fainted, honey." Fran ran a warm washcloth over my sweaty forehead.

"For how long?"

"Less than a minute. Just lie here and don't try to get up just yet."

I fainted? I'd never fainted in my life. As my body functions returned to normal, the reason behind my incident became all too clear.

I knew that top name on the list.

Rosalee Black.

Oh, my God.

"Honey, are you going to be okay? Do we need to call 911?" Fran and Howard leaned over me, both their faces lined with concern.

"No, no. I'll be okay once the shock wears off."

"You saw something. What was it?"

I closed my eyes to buy time, faking that I was resting. I didn't want to tell her. She'd hate me. So would Howard. How could they not hate me? I'd lived a lie for six-plus years and hadn't realized it. But my ignorance was no excuse for a cold, hard fact I should've seen. Neither child looked like Mark.

They looked like...

Him.

I'd never given it much thought. Never once questioned how Mark and I had the athletic ability of a slug, while the children were insanely talented athletes, even at their young age. And they were both natural-born skaters.

Of course they were.

"Caro, honey, are you okay?"

My eyes fluttered open, and I focused on those two worried faces in my line of vision. I had to tell them before they did their own research and figured it out. I wouldn't let that happen. This was my story to tell, my transgression to admit.

"That summer I graduated a year early from high school, and Mark went to Europe, we broke up for a few months."

"Yes, we remember." Fran's gaze darted quickly to Howard and back to me.

"I met someone when I was working at the skating rink. He was there for a summer hockey program for talented junior players. His name was Easton Black." My heart pounded in my chest as I waited for their reaction.

"Black?" Howard's voice cracked slightly, and he sat down hard on the coffee table. Good thing he was a slight man, or he'd have broken the thing in two.

"The first name on the list was Rosalee Black." Fran stated what we all knew, but I was relieved I didn't have to explain further.

"His mother."

"Mark isn't the father of the twins?" Fran stood and backed away from me as if I were carrying a highly contagious disease. She held her hands over her mouth and stared.

"It appears not." I sat up slowly, needing to face these two people from a sitting position. "I am so sorry. I never knew. Mark and I got back together within a week of Easton leaving, and I...I didn't know. You must think I'm a horrible person." I buried my face in my hands, and the tears came and wouldn't stop. I cried with huge sobs shaking my body. At some point in time, Fran sat next to me, and Howard sat on the other side of me. Fran rubbed my back, and both said nothing.

"Do you hate me?" I asked finally. These two were all I had in this world except for my kids and my best friend, Juniper.

"No, honey, we don't hate you," Fran insisted, but her gaze was full of confusion and uncertainty.

"You made a mistake, but that doesn't mean we stopped loving you. We'll get through this together." Howard was in his take-charge mode, and I was fine with that.

I didn't deserve the love of these people. They'd already forgiven me for passing my children off as their son's children, not that I'd intentionally done it, but in my mind, ignorance was no excuse.

"What do we do now?" I said.

"Easton needs to know. It's the right thing to do. He's their father." Howard looked to Fran for confirmation, and she nodded. Despite the shock of a few minutes ago, they'd both recovered remarkably and were already looking to the future.

I was stuck in the present and the past.

I had to tell Easton. I didn't have an option.

It was the right thing to do.

Chapter Four

HOLDING ALL THE CARDS

--Easton--

*T*hat next morning, Coach Gorst called me into his office. It was a typical rainy day in Seattle. Leaves were turning colors and covering the sidewalks, soon to give way to an oppressive gray that would dominate the next several months. In a few days, the regular hockey season began, and I wanted to be on this team so badly I could taste it.

As I was going into the coach's office, Axel walked out. His head was down, and he didn't glance in my direction, but he mumbled, "Good luck."

I grimaced and braced myself for the news. Up until I'd seen the devastated expression on Axel's face, I'd been confident I'd made the team, but that very confidence eroded with every passing minute. My preseason play was as good as any rookie's, and better than many of the veterans' performances. I'd done everything asked of me by the coaching staff, laying my heart and body on the line to make this team.

Getting sent down wouldn't be the end of the world and only

meant a player needed more development time, but I'd wanted to be one of those guys who didn't have that happen. Besides, in my way of thinking, I was already behind most of my peers. I'd played four years of college hockey and had sat out an additional year for an injury, which equated to more development time than most of the players in rookie camp. Five years spent at the college level. In some ways, maybe I'd been stupid to go that route, but at the same time, I knew in my heart I'd done the right thing for me. The injury had shown me I had what it took to come back and deal with adversity.

Drawing in a deep breath, I steeled myself for whatever was to come and opened the door.

Coach Gorst glanced up from his computer monitor and waved me toward a seat. "Be right with you, Easton." He tapped on his keyboard for a very long, excruciating minute. I studied his face, but he gave nothing away.

Gorst was relatively young in the world of NHL coaches. I doubted he was even forty yet. When he'd been hired by the Sockeyes four years ago, his coaching methods had been progressive and unorthodox. With the success he'd had, including winning the Cup last season, many other teams duplicated his approach to coaching.

He was fiery, tough, and had high expectations. He was known for his ability to get the best out of his players by capitalizing on their strengths and improving on their weaknesses. He emphasized basics, such as good skating and using your edges like a figure skater did. He even employed figure skaters to teach the finer points of skating.

I'd been the model student for Gorst's teachings, never complaining and always giving 100 percent, yet here I was, worried I might not make the team. I clasped my hands in my lap, gripping them so hard that I was cutting off the circulation. Loosening up the viselike hold, I took a few deep, calming breaths.

And waited.

Gorst looked up and pushed his chair away from his desk. He rose and crossed from behind the desk to sit next to me at the small conference table in his office. There were a few short raps on his door, and he shouted, "Come in."

Team captain Isaac "Ice" Wolfe entered the room and took a seat next to Gorst. His face wore its usual stone-cold expression. He'd earned his nickname. I couldn't recall him smiling once during our entire training camp. Usually, he was scowling.

"Easton, your stats are some of the best in the nation for a rookie. Hell, even for a veteran." Gorst's words almost seemed rehearsed.

Did I hear a *but* in there? I tamped down my growing excitement and forced a neutral expression on my face. Now my fingernails were digging painfully into my palms, but the pain didn't distract me from this man who would set the course for my future with his next words. I glanced at Ice, who scrutinized me intently, as if gauging any signs of weakness. His scrutiny only amped up my nervousness. I was sweating now. If they kept me in suspense much longer, sweat would be trickling down my brow.

"You've become a valuable member of this team in a surprisingly short time," Gorst continued, then gave Ice a nod. Being valuable had to be a good thing, didn't it?

Ice cleared his throat. Was I hallucinating, or was there a ghost of a smile on his face? "I've watched you develop throughout training camp. You keep your head down, work hard, don't cause any problems. You're a good teammate, and I'd be proud to play beside you."

"Thank, uh, thank you." I was fucking going to faint. I put my hands, palms down, on the table to steady myself as my world began to tilt and lurch like a carnival ride badly in need of repair.

"Welcome to the Sockeyes." Gorst ended my torture and stood. He held out his hand. I hauled myself to my feet and shook his offered hand. They were smiling, both of them, and all the tension poured out of me.

"Thank you. Thank you. Thank you." I was gushing, but neither man appeared to mind.

Ice shook my hand next. His grip was strong and sure. "Congratulations, Big E. You earned it."

I opened my mouth to say thank you again and snapped it shut. Ice was a man of few words, so I nodded instead.

"Do you have any questions for us?" Gorst asked.

"Uh, not right now. I can't think of any."

"Good then. Stop by personnel and fill out the necessary paperwork. We'll be seeing you on the ice."

I'd been dismissed, and I wasn't about to overstay my welcome. I hurried for the door, tripping over a chair leg in the process, and flailed my arms to get my balance. Reaching the door, I let myself out without looking back. I was too elated to be embarrassed.

I wanted to race down the hallways shouting out my good fortune to the rooftops. Instead, I forced myself to walk slowly to the elevator. I hadn't planned it, but seconds later, I stood in the empty locker room in front of the stall with my name on it. My stall. I was a Sockeye. I was a professional hockey player.

The first thing I was going to do was make an appointment for one of those fish tattoos all the guys sported. Then I was calling my mother and my two hockey-playing brothers.

Tonight, I was celebrating.

For a moment, my joy was dampened when I realized my best buddy on this team, Axel, wouldn't be celebrating with me. I'd still invite him, of course. He was young. He'd make it. Guys got traded, or injuries prevented them from taking the ice. Not that I'd wish an injury on anyone, but that shit did happen.

I dialed my mother. Mom was as excited as I was. Mom had been the consummate hockey mom after my dad had died and she'd been forced to raise us on her own. She'd gone to every game when we were kids, not an easy feat considering there were three of us, but she managed to juggle her responsibilities and support us at the same time. She was a computer programmer and made pretty good money.

My brother Zane was starting his third year in the league. My younger brother, Max, played junior hockey and lived at home. Mom would tell Max.

After I hung up with Mom, I called Zane. He answered on the first ring as if he'd been waiting for my call. "Well?" he said, not giving me a chance to say hello, how are you, or fuck you.

"I'm a Sockeye," I blurted out. Zane let out a whoop, enjoying this moment almost as much as I did. I heard him say something and then heard clapping.

"Where are you?"

"I'm having lunch with some of the guys. We're all happy for you."

"I did it. I really did it. I'd worried so much my choice to go to college might screw with my ability to make a team, but in the end those five years didn't hurt me one bit."

"You made the right choice for you, E."

"I did," I said proudly. I could've followed in Zane's footsteps and gone the major-junior route. Things had worked out great for him. Now they were working out for me.

All those hours of practicing, playing through injuries, and sacrifice culminated in this moment. I'd worked my entire life to be here and allowed nothing and no one to stand in my way.

Chapter Five

JUST DO IT

--Caroline--

*I*t'd been a month since I'd gotten the devastating news from the DNA test. I hadn't talked to Easton yet; instead I'd worried myself into an absolute frenzy of fear, dread, and loathing of my own shortcomings. I conjured up all kinds of scenarios in my head, and most of them weren't good. What if Easton didn't want to know his kids? Even worse, what if he took me to court for custody? I'd never have enough money to fight him legally. What if? What if? What if?

No matter what, I knew I had to tell him. My life had been put on hold until I told him, as had Fran and Howard's. They weren't leaving me for their well-deserved retirement until we'd resolved this. And what would be the resolution? Once Fran and Howard left, there was nothing to keep me here. I had so many questions and zero answers.

I was still amazed they'd forgiven me as fully as they had, a testament to what good people they were.

I'd left Hailey with Fran and Howard to fill the role of hockey mom and shuttle Heath to practice. I searched the group of kids skating around the rink, easily picking out my son. He was bigger than most his age, with a determination not usually present in children so young. So much like his father. I didn't know why I hadn't seen the similarities before.

Heath had dark hair and eyes. Ice skating and hockey were his jam. He looked like Easton. Hailey, on the other hand, favored me—small and petite with blonde curls. She was all girl, loving pink and figure skating.

Heath glanced up as he streaked by, intent on his skating. His face was the picture of ultimate concentration as he focused on the puck.

After taking out my ever-present day planner, I opened it and wrote a few notes of things to do later this evening once I'd put the children to bed. The first thing I wrote was *Call Easton*. I'd called the number he'd had that summer several times, and each time, I'd ended the call before the first ring.

Heath fought for the puck with another kid, and the two of them went down still battling it out. The coaches separated them, and Heath sprang to his feet, looking triumphant. I frowned. As the mother of a child who'd just gotten in a fight, I wasn't thrilled, but my baby boy was ecstatic. He skated toward me with a broad smile on his face. When he saw me smiling back, he frowned and looked away.

Since his father, Mark, had died, the only place Heath seemed happy was on the ice. Sometimes I swore he personally blamed me for Mark's death. I guess it was easier to hoist your frustration and grief on the one who loved you most, knowing they'd be there no matter what.

He skated past me and along the boards. The kid he'd scuffled with caught up to him, and they talked and laughed as they skated, their differences already forgotten. Kids were like that. I wish adults were better at forgetting the bad things.

I wish I was.

He came around again and waved his stick at the coach, grinning with that one dimple, a dimple so much like someone else's my heart thudded longingly in my chest.

Longingly?

This had to stop. Easton might be the father of my children, but we weren't anything to each other. He'd broken my heart all those years ago, and I'd made a promise to myself that I'd never allow a man like him the ability to hurt me again. He'd not just hurt me, he'd destroyed me with his callous words the last night we were together.

Shaking off the memories, I concentrated on my son, even as the similarities made it increasingly difficult to banish Easton from my thoughts.

An hour later, I pulled up to Fran and Howard's house, noticing a For Sale sign in the front yard. That was new. Momentary panic grabbed me, but I shoved it away. I was happy for them. They were moving on, as I needed to move on.

As soon as I neared the front door, Hailey burst out the front door of her grandparents' house and streaked across the lawn. Her long blonde hair streamed behind her, and she threw herself into my arms. I picked her up and hugged her tightly. She squealed and wriggled out of my arms, turning to her brother with a nonstop flood of words. He stared impassively at her and headed into the house, his sister hot on his tail and talking a million miles a minute.

Minutes later, they were seated at the breakfast nook, eating some of Fran's savory stew. Fran and I sat in the living room, while Howard watched sports on TV. Howard loved sports. It didn't matter what kind.

"I saw the For Sale sign."

"It's time, honey. We have to sell this place. We'd both promised each other months ago that we wouldn't spend another cold winter in Illinois. Besides, we can't afford the payments on both houses."

"I'm happy for you. I really am."

Fran studied me with troubled eyes. "What will you do? Where will you go?"

"I don't know yet. I'm not staying here. I need a fresh start."

"You can always join us in Arizona."

The invitation was beyond tempting, yet I'd never wanted to live in Arizona. I didn't like really hot places. I was a Chicago girl and didn't mind the cold.

Fran shrugged at my lack of response. "Whatever you decide, we're here for you. You know that. Have you given any thought to getting a nursing degree?"

I hadn't. Not really. The only thing I'd come up with was to start as a nurse's aide and figure it out from there. Sadly, a nurse's aide salary would make it difficult to comfortably support two young children on a single income, let alone save money for nursing school.

I was the queen of indecision, and I was running out of time and money. I had to choose a direction and work toward whatever goal I set.

"Have you called Easton yet?" Fran asked.

Ah, there was the elephant in the room. They'd left me alone about Easton, but now the pressure was on. The Mills' house was on the market, and they'd no longer be available to be my crutch.

I shook my head, glancing briefly at Fran and looking away, ashamed of my cowardice. I cringed at the censure on her face. I'd disappointed her one more time. Avoiding the inevitable was no longer working for me.

"I'll call him tonight after the kids are tucked in."

"I'm going to hold you to it. No more putting it off." Fran's determined expression didn't allow any argument. Tonight was the night.

--Easton--

We were one month into the regular season. I was playing well on the third line, might even be moved up to second. I'd scored a couple NHL goals and had multiple assists. Everything was going my way, yet I couldn't shake this funk I was in.

Kaden, Steele, and I had leased a condo overlooking Lake Union within easy walking distance of the practice facility. It came fully furnished, and we didn't add any personal touches to the place. Steele was a neat freak and always picking up our crap, while Kaden and I cared less about a tidy home. We did have a housekeeper come in once a week to do the deep cleaning. All in all, we were three bachelors living the good life.

After practice, I didn't leave the ice when the rest of my teammates did. I stayed and skated along the boards at a leisurely pace, hands behind my back. I concentrated on the feel of my blades sliding along the slick surface, listened to the swish-swish sound, and tried to find the zone, which had eluded me recently. Skating had always been a form of meditation for me, but lately not so much. I stopped and stared upward at the Sockeyes logo on the wall in the practice facility.

Being here had been my goal, but now that I'd reached the top of the pile, I was vaguely disappointed. What was wrong with me? Why couldn't I shake the feeling something was missing?

With a sigh, I skated off the ice. By the time I entered the locker room, everyone had left. I changed into street clothes but didn't want to go home just yet.

I wandered around the team lounge, watched some game tape, and felt totally lost and alone. I slumped down in a chair and hugged my coffee cup, staring out the bank of windows at the Space Needle nearby.

I'd been out a little too late last night, drunk too much, and now I was paying for it. I'd been sluggish in practice, and the coaches had noticed. Cousin Coop had ridden my ass, constantly bitching at me. He was hardest on me, probably because he expected more from me and to prove he wasn't showing favoritism.

The door opened, but I didn't look up. I wasn't in the mood for company. Hopefully, if I ignored whoever it was, they'd go away.

"You don't seem overly happy for a rookie who's taking the NHL by storm." Ice sat down next to me at a table in the team lounge.

I glanced up at my captain, ready to deny I was anything but ecstatic, only no words came. Ice didn't tolerate bullshit, and by the look on his face, any protest on my part would be just that. He saw right through me. The room was empty. I doubted anyone else would be crazy enough to be at the practice facility after the practice we'd had. They'd scattered to nurse their wounds or drink them into oblivion.

I needed someone to talk to. I didn't dare talk to cousin Coop. He was in his first year of coaching and super-focused on doing a good job himself. He wouldn't understand why I was feeling anything but giddy.

"You noticed?" I said.

"I notice everything." Ice took a sip of his coffee and studied me without saying a word.

"I don't want to sound like I'm an entitled, ungrateful asshole."

"Well, we all sound like that at times, so fess up. What's going on?" Ice wasn't the touchy-feely type, nor was he talkative. The fact that he was sitting here with me having a conversation that didn't focus on hockey was highly unusual. He was the captain, and he took it seriously, so he was doing his job. I tried not to read any more into his concern than an overall interest in his team's well-being.

"I don't know. I feel off. I thought making it to the NHL would be everything I'd ever dreamed of. I've worked so hard for this. Now that I'm here, I'm looking around and wondering shouldn't there be more? I'm empty inside. Something's missing, and I'm pissed at myself that hockey isn't enough. Don't get me wrong, I love hockey. I live for hockey, but there has to be more, doesn't there? I gave up a lot to be here." I hadn't planned on dumping on him like that, but the words came out before I could stop them.

He considered my words for several seconds before speaking. "Did you give up someone special?" he guessed. The hard lines of his face softened slightly.

I blinked a few times, ready to deny his claim, then really thought about it. "I don't know."

He nodded sagely, as if he understood totally. I knew he was madly in love with his wife. Whenever she was in the room, this enigmatic, hard-to-read man turned into a sappy, lovesick fool.

"There was this girl when I was sixteen, had two years left of high school. I walked away from her, thinking hockey was all I needed. I tracked her down a couple years ago. She's married with kids, and I can't stop thinking her husband has my life, the life I should've had. It's weird."

"It's not weird. All the money and fame and even your passion for hockey don't mean much without someone to share it with. Take it from a guy who knows."

"Do you ever wonder about the road not taken?" I asked him.

"Not much anymore because the road I travelled ended up being the best journey I could imagine, and I wouldn't change a thing, not even the painful parts, because it got me where I am today. She's your past. You need to live your present. There'll be someone else, someone even more perfect for you. You have to believe in fate. When you're least looking for love, it finds you."

Well, I wasn't looking. I must've been gaping at him with an open mouth and something akin to shock because he chuckled.

"If you tell anyone about this conversation, I'll kick your ass," he said.

"Don't worry, I wouldn't dream of it."

With a nod, he stood and left the room. I watched him go, deep in thought. I was twenty-three. I was a Puck Brother, for fuck's sake. I didn't need a woman to complete me or nag at me or try to control me. This entire conversation with Ice had been like something out of those old *Twilight Zone* shows Steele liked to watch.

What the fuck was wrong with me?

I didn't know why I wasn't enjoying the rookie experience as much as I should be, but that emptiness inside me had nothing to do with a woman. Maybe more like wanting something I couldn't have. Some deeply buried part of me had always assumed Caro would be waiting when I chose to come back and claim her.

The entire thing had been eating at me lately, and my feelings on the matter were ludicrous.

With a sigh, I pushed to my feet. Time to go home and see what culinary delight Kaden had concocted. The man could cook.

I walked wearily to my truck. I did need a nap.

I slipped into the leather seat of my Chevy 2500HD and started the engine. It purred like the finely tuned machine it was. I don't know why I bought this truck. It wasn't like I pulled a trailer or hauled heavy shit with it. My ego must've been talking when I'd gone car shopping after getting my signing bonus.

I went home to the condo and hung out with Steele for the night, playing video games and watching a game.

I was about to call it a night when my phone rang. I frowned at the device. When someone called this late, it wasn't necessarily good. Maybe one of the Puck Bros had been arrested and needed bailed out.

I picked it up. Not recognizing the number, I considered letting it go to voicemail, but I was inexplicably compelled to answer that call.

"Yeah?" I said, waiting to chew some solicitor's ass. A long silence followed. I almost hung up but didn't.

"Easton?" The hesitant female voice struck a nerve deep inside me, bringing back melancholy memories of another time and place. I knew that voice, but I was in denial.

"Yeah." Suspicion crept into my tone. Had some recent one-night stand managed to get my phone number? There'd been a few. Not a lot, but enough to keep my standing as a Puck Brother intact.

"It's—it's Caroline. Caroline Mills, uh, Jones."

I gaped at the phone as if I expected a monster to emerge from the screen and swallow me in one big gulp. My palm was sweaty, and the device started to slip from my hand. I fumbled to catch it before it hit the floor.

Caroline?

I gripped the phone until my knuckles were white. My breathing was rapid and shallow like I was about to have a fucking panic attack or exhibit some stupid wussy behavior my teammates would be appalled to witness. A quick glance around the room didn't reveal my roommates had appeared out of the woodwork to witness my loss of composure and near breakdown. I unclenched my hand from the phone before I crushed it. My fucking hands were shaking. My forehead had broken out in a sweat.

I had to be coming down with the flu. A voice from the past wouldn't affect me like this.

I cleared my throat, praying my tone didn't betray my emotions, uh, correction, the state of my health. "Caro, what a surprise."

I gave myself a mental pat on the back. I'd given nothing away.

"I'm sure it is."

"How did you get my number?" I wondered out loud.

"It's the same one you had back when we...we were friends."

"Friends?" I barked out a disbelieving laugh. We'd been way more than friends that summer, and my depraved mind immediately conjured up images of Caro's gorgeous body naked in the moonlight. I swallowed hard and couldn't stop my dick from responding to those memories.

Our passion had been hot and blinding. Judging by the difficulty I'd had wiping her from my thoughts recently, also epically memorable.

"Yes, we were friends." Her accusing words cut deep. She was right. We'd been more than fuck buddies. We'd been each other's confidants and sounding boards. We'd spent hours talking about our hopes and dreams. She'd planned on attending nursing school in the fall. I had two more years of school and would be going the college route to further my hockey career.

I'd ended it badly with her. Instead of making promises I couldn't keep, I'd been bluntly honest and told her we were too young, had no future, and had a great time while it lasted. I'd cut her loose and myself, never telling her I loved her, because at sixteen, I didn't know what love was.

I'd been an ass, and I still saw the stricken look on her face. She'd recovered quickly and shot back with her own biting words about what a jerk I was, and she'd be glad to be rid of me.

I'd blown it. I felt a twinge of jealousy that what her husband had should've—could've—been mine.

"Easton, I need to talk to you. In person."

"You do?"

"Tell me when, and I'll come to you."

She was willing to come to Seattle? I recovered quickly. "All right. I don't have a game on Sunday. Where would you like to meet?" I controlled my tone, coming off as all businesslike and suppressing the hundred questions scrolling through my head.

"I don't know Seattle."

"I'll text you a location. Does seven p.m. on Sunday work for you?"

"Yeah. Thank you, Easton. I know this must seem weird."

She was right about that. We said our goodbyes, and I was left with those hundred questions and not one answer.

Chapter Six

THE HARDEST THING

--Caroline--

*F*acing him after all these years would be the hardest thing I'd ever had to do. I didn't know what to expect. No doubt my news would come as a shock. Would he be angry, be in denial, or walk away and never look back? All worst-case scenarios. In fact, I'd made a list last night of the best and worst things that could happen when I told him. Then I'd written notes on what I wanted to say and gone over them several times in an attempt to memorize them.

Right now, I couldn't remember one word of my speech.

I'd considered the cowardly way out by having an attorney contact him, but he deserved more than that. Besides, the money for a retainer wasn't in my budget.

I was early and took a seat in a semiprivate booth near the back. I ordered a glass of wine to help calm my nerves. Fidgeting with the stem of the wineglass, I turned it in slow circles, mesmerized by the golden liquid sloshing in the glass. The movement was calming.

A hand touched my back, startling me. The wineglass tipped and spilled wine across the table and down the thighs of my skinny jeans. I stared at the growing patch of wetness in horror. When I heard a familiar chuckle, my eyes were drawn to the sparkling brown eyes of the boy—make that man—I'd spent one hot, memorable summer with.

Without a word, Easton hustled to the bar and grabbed a couple towels. He handed one to me and mopped up the wine on the table with the other. The cocktail waitress hurried over and finished the job, bringing me another glass of wine.

"Do you have a sippy cup?" Easton joked to the waitress, ignoring my scathing glare. She stared at him as if she were in a trance, sucked in by the same brilliant smile and dazzling good looks that'd pulled me under their spell years ago.

"I'm sure I can find something," she gushed.

"I'm fine, thank you," I shot back primly.

Easton shrugged. "I'll have an IPA. Whatever you have on tap."

"Absolutely." This woman was practically eating him alive with her eyes. A rush of jealousy caught me off guard as I recalled all the girls hanging on him and chasing after him back when we were an item.

I didn't like it then, and I didn't like it much now either. I had no claim on this man, and I didn't want one. My sole purpose was to do the right thing, even if I feared the consequences.

He took the seat across from me just as his beer was delivered. The waitress didn't leave but lingered, staring longingly at Easton. He nodded at her, and she finally took the hint, slinking away.

"You look good," he said as his gaze ran over me. Every cell in my body lit up from the inside out. Our eyes met, and all those years melted away. We were two people who enjoyed each other's company and each other's bodies.

He was older. His face had none of a boy's softness but was all angular lines and hard planes. His dark hair was unruly as always, and that same lock fell over his forehead. I resisted the urge to brush it back as I often had. His dark eyes still shone with humor and good nature.

Realizing I was staring, I forced my gaze away from his hypnotic brown eyes. I picked up the wineglass and it started to slip from my moist fingers. Easton grabbed it before I spilled another glass all over the table and him.

His eyes twinkled with mischief as he handed the wine back to me. "About that sippy cup?"

"I don't need one," I responded with a ghost of a smile on my lips.

"Coulda fooled me."

I took a sip and placed the glass on the table. Digging deep for the courage I'd need to bring up this subject, I dived in. "I suppose you're wondering why you're here."

He nodded.

I started fingering the stem of the wineglass again, ignoring a dramatic gasp from him.

"Easton, there's no easy way to say this."

"Then just say it." Life was simple like that to him. Black and white. No shades of gray. I, on the other hand, worried too much and fretted about upsetting others. There wasn't any getting around this. He was going to be upset. "Or you could make a list?" he quipped with a teasing grin.

I didn't smile back. I forced my gaze to meet his and blurted out the words, my carefully written speech all but forgotten. "You're a father."

He'd just brought his beer to his lips, and he choked on it. The glass slipped from his grasp, hit the edge of the table, and sprayed all over both of us before crashing to the ground and splintering into a million pieces. The attention of every patron in the place was drawn to our table, followed by gasps as the crowd recognized one of the newest members of their defending Stanley Cup champions.

Easton didn't notice the mess or the gathering crowd of people. He gaped at me in utter, absolute shock. The staff rushed to clean up the mess, and I slid out of the booth so they could wipe it down. As the crowd converged on us, they blocked my view of Easton.

I took advantage of the chaos and bolted for freedom.

--Easton--

In the ensuing melee of fans begging for my autograph and staff scrubbing the booth and floor, I lost sight of Caro. When things finally calmed down, she was nowhere to be found.

She'd hit me with a bombshell and fled like the guilty party that she was. I had a child? I was a father?

I pushed past the remaining fans, tossed a fifty on the counter for my drinks and uneaten dinner, and dashed out the door. No sign of her in the parking lot. She was long gone.

Maybe her disappearance was for the best. I needed alone time to process my change in status from single guy with zero attachment to single father.

What the fuck?

Anger replaced confusion as I drove out of the bar parking lot. She'd dumped this on me and disappeared, offering no details. Did I have a son or a daughter? How old was he or she? How did Caro know I was the father? Why was she telling me this now?

I did the math in my head. My child should be around six years old. It'd been over seven years since that summer we spent together.

Why hadn't she told me she was pregnant?

My mind raced back in time, running through that last conversation when I'd dumped her. She'd been devastated, and it hadn't been easy on me either. Had she known then?

What kind of mother waited seven years to tell a father he had a child? I missed all those years. I was angry and hurt, along with confused. I itched to call her back, but I had to calm down first. Think about what she'd said, which was very little. Being a father wasn't anything I'd considered. I was pretty good with kids, but having one of my own was far different than coaching a group of kids.

Those two children I'd seen outside her house...was one of them mine? I searched my memory for images of them, but I'd been so caught up in seeing her again, I had very little recollection beyond a blonde-haired girl and a dark-haired boy.

I drove home despite not wanting to answer a bunch of questions from a nosy Kaden or endure a penetrating and all-knowing stare from

Steele. Regardless, I had to talk to someone, and they were my someones.

I walked into the condo, praying they weren't partying and were relatively sober. I wasn't in the mood for drunks. Instead, I heard the crashing of pots and pans in the kitchen and smelled the aroma of baking cookies. Kaden was at it again. The man loved to cook, and he loved to eat. I guess one of his parents was a chef.

I followed my nose into the kitchen, which was a disaster. Kaden had a habit of using every available pan and utensil when he cooked. Steele, our resident neat freak, was trying to clean up, but Kaden was messing shit up as fast as Steele could clean it. If I hadn't been traumatized by Caro's revelation, I'd be snorting with laughter at the two of them.

They didn't need one more ass in the kitchen, so I sat on a barstool at the counter and snagged a warm chocolate chip cookie from the dozen cooling on wax paper. Despite the evening's earlier news flash, I allowed myself a moment to savor the warm cookie oozing with melted chocolate chips.

"Help yourself," Kaden said sarcastically.

"Like you were going to eat all these?" I shot back.

"The team captains want them for the road trip tomorrow." Kaden sighed and spooned piles of dough onto a cookie sheet. The life of a rookie. We were subjected to the whims of veterans and their stomachs. On the last road trip, the captains decided they wanted our seats, and we were stuck with seats up front with the coaches. Now every time we got on the plane, no matter where we sat, they demanded our seats.

I grabbed another cookie, ignoring my bud's deepening scowl. Steele wiped the soap off his hands and crossed the kitchen to take the stool next to mine. He grabbed a cookie for himself.

"Give up?" I asked Steele.

"No point in cleaning up until he's finished his destruction."

"My thought exactly."

"Where've you been?" Kaden asked as he bent over to check the cookies in the oven.

"Meeting a girlfriend from my past."

Kaden and Steele exchanged glances. Both sets of brows shot upward, but they said nothing.

"The one that got away. The one I can't seem to forget." I was stupid to admit such a thing to these clowns. They'd surely use the information against me sometime in the future.

Steele's brows crept up farther into his hairline. Kaden frowned, not sure what to think of my statement.

"Where's she living?" Steele said.

"I'm not sure."

"Does she want to get back together?" Kaden narrowed his eyes.

"I'm not interested in a long-term relationship with her or anyone else, but there are complications I didn't know about until now."

"Complications?" they both stated at the same time. Kaden pulled the next sheet of cookies from the oven and grabbed the batch ready to be baked.

"Yeah, a complication. I'm a father."

Steele spit out his cookie, and Kaden dropped the cookie sheet full of raw cookies on the floor.

"What the fuck?" Kaden blinked several times and stepped over the mess to stand across the counter from me. His mouth moved, but nothing came out, as if he couldn't quite figure out which question to ask first.

"A father?" Steele shook his head over and over, as if the motion would help him make sense of my words.

"Yeah, a father." I held up my hand to stop the questions from coming. "I was so shocked, I dropped my beer. It drenched us, and the glass broke on the floor."

"No wonder you stink like stale beer," Kaden said.

"And look like you should've been wearing a diaper," Steele added.

"Yeah, thanks. Anyway, in the ensuing chaos, she slipped out."

"She dropped a bomb like that on you and left? What the fuck?" Steele shook his head and scowled. Steele rarely showed emotion, so this display was epic and somewhat touching. I'd never point that out to him though. He'd be mortified.

"She told you that you're a father and then vanished?"

"Sure did." Anger seeped into my tone and vibrated through my body. The anger kept the confusion and guilt at bay. If I stayed pissed at her, I wouldn't have to accept my responsibility in this situation. After all, there wasn't any excuse for what she'd done.

"I have zero respect for any woman who keeps a baby secret from the father. We have as much rights as they do when it comes to being parents." Steele pounded his fist on the table. Kaden and I stared at this stranger. We'd never seen him so adamant about a subject other than hockey. There had to be a story there.

"I agree," Kaden said. "What are you going to do about it?"

"Call her back and demand an explanation," I answered.

"Get a DNA test. She might be trying to extort money from you." Kaden was ever the suspicious one when it came to women. There was a story there, too. I guess we all had our own secrets. Hell, I had a secret I hadn't even known about.

"I will. Tomorrow."

"Are you in love with this woman?" By the horrified expression on Kaden's face, he couldn't think of anything worse than falling in love.

"I...uh, no, it was a summer fling. A fucking memorable summer fling. I dumped her and walked away. On a whim, I looked her up a few years ago and found out she was married with kids."

"Why is a married woman looking you up and claiming you're a father?"

"Lots of questions. No fucking answers."

"Be careful, E, something seems off," Kaden warned.

"Get a good attorney," Steele added.

I nodded. Tomorrow morning, I'd straighten out this mess.

Not that I'd be able to get one minute of sleep.

I was a fucking *father*. How did a guy handle news like that seven years too late?

Chapter Seven

THE TRUTH

--Easton--

*I*f I had a child, I had to know. I wasn't sure what I'd do with that knowledge, but I would do right by the kid. Caro was married, and most likely the child thought Caro's husband was his or her father. I wondered if this man knew about me. I couldn't fathom why she was contacting me after keeping the secret for seven years unless it all came back to money. Her timing was suspect. I was an NHL player and making an NHL salary. Caro and her husband might want a piece of that pie to enhance their quality of living.

If the child was mine, I had every intention of owning up to my responsibilities. Beyond that, I hadn't a clue. I was twenty-three years old and not ready to be a dad. I was still growing up myself.

I admitted with a twinge of guilt that Caro hadn't been given that choice. If the child was mine, she'd have given birth at eighteen. Then I reminded myself I'd have been involved if I'd known.

I wondered as I had a thousand times since last night if I had a son or daughter. Did the kid look anything like me? Did my child like to skate and have any athletic ability? Caro had been the least-athletic person I'd ever met. She could trip over a leaf and fall flat on her face, but she'd known her hockey. She'd loved hockey. We'd spent hours talking about it, and she'd never once been bored with it.

As mad as I was at Caro, I couldn't help thinking about how good she'd looked. She might have given birth, but she'd maintained her trim figure. Her honey-blonde hair had still been long and glossy. Her eyes had been as blue as I remembered, so blue I could lose myself for hours in them. I hadn't seen her smile, but she'd once had a hundred-megawatt smile that lit up any room. She'd stirred something deep inside me, something I'd prefer to keep buried. My body had responded to her presence, her scent, her closeness, even though I didn't want it to.

Memories of the summer we spent together came rushing back. I'd fallen for her with all the passion and hormones of a teenage boy. Those strong emotions had scared the crap out of me, and I'd mistaken them for love. I'd torn out of there, far and fast, to get away from my own feelings.

And now she'd kept the ultimate secret from me. I didn't know if I'd ever forgive her for such a thing, but I wouldn't have to. She was married to another man. All we needed to do was straighten out this parenting business and figure out what rights I wanted to enforce and how the kid fit into my life.

Caro had texted me a few times to apologize for her rapid retreat. I recalled what a worrier she was, and my lack of response would've given her plenty to worry about.

At six a.m., I picked up my phone, found her last text, and texted her back.

--Caroline--

I woke early in the morning in a strange hotel room. I hadn't fallen asleep until the wee hours, and I'd spent a good part of the evening fretting. Had I misjudged Easton? Was he disinterested in being a father? Did he hate me for running and not explaining the situation?

From his point of view, I didn't look like a very good person. I'd regretted my rash actions and returned to the bar only to find him gone. I'd texted him several times, the last being at midnight, with no answer. I checked my phone almost every hour to find nothing.

I wished I'd allowed Fran to come to Seattle with me. She'd offered, but deep down, I knew this was something I had to do myself. I'd sure messed that up. Fran would tell me to have patience. I'd dropped a bombshell on Easton, and he needed time to put all of this in perspective.

Knowing it was early, I called Fran. She wouldn't mind, even if I woke her up, and I needed to speak to someone. Fran was the closest thing I had to a real mother.

"Caro? Is everything okay?" Fran's voice was a mixture of sleepiness and alarm.

"It's okay. I'm sorry to wake you up."

"You don't have to apologize. We've been waiting for your call. When I said I was here for you, I meant it, no matter the time. Tell me what's going on."

I quickly ran through the events of last night, and Fran listened without comment until I finished. "And you haven't heard a word since?"

"It's still early." I sighed, feeling both defeated and relieved. If Easton didn't want any part of his children, I'd go on with my life, raise my kids, and work on a career path.

"I'm sure you will this morning. Give him time to adjust."

"Maybe I'd just as soon he didn't call back. Maybe it's better that way. The kids can continue to believe Mark is their bio father. I won't have to worry about Easton wanting custody down the road or inter-fering with my parenting..."

"Take it from someone who's been down that road and has deep regrets. Even if Easton doesn't want a relationship with his children, you can't keep this secret from them like I did from Mark. They have a right to know when they're old enough."

"Even if he doesn't care?"

"Absolutely. For all the reasons we did those DNA tests. People need to know where they came from and about their genetics. It's important."

More so to her than to me, but I couldn't discount my children might also want to know and had that right. "I guess I'll fly home and wait to hear from him."

"Stay a few more days. Give him a little time."

That was the last thing I wanted to do. I preferred slinking off in the inky black Seattle night with the hope he'd forget all about me as he had the last seven years. And to think I'd once believed I loved him.

Even worse, seeing him again had dredged up feelings best buried. Easton and I still had chemistry, but he'd broken my heart once, and he wouldn't get a second chance, even if he wanted one—which I was damn sure he didn't.

Fran and I spoke for a few more minutes about the kids and ended the call. I placed the phone on the nightstand and leaned back against the bed. I closed my eyes, but all I saw was the shock on Easton's face when I told him he was a father.

My cell chirped, signaling a text message.

With shaking hands, I picked up my cell phone. Only a few people had my new number, and Easton was one of those few.

Meet me at Lake Union Park at eight a.m. near the Seattle ferry dock.

My throat was dry, and I swallowed hard. With trembling fingers, I texted him back.

OK.

That was it. He didn't respond. I stared at the phone as if the device held all the answers.

--Easton--

I arrived a half hour early at the park. I sat down at a picnic table and immediately regretted it. My efforts to look casual were now thwarted by a wet ass from a soaked picnic bench thanks to a recent shower.

With a sigh, I ignored the big spot on the back of my jeans and stayed seated. The last thing I wanted was for Caro to pick up on how anxious I was.

I wiped my palms on my thighs and took a gulp from the water bottle I'd brought along. I wished I'd brought a flask of whiskey, but it was too early to drink, even for me.

I had a child, and I was both dying and dreading to learn the details.

A car pulled into the parking lot several yards away. It was a nondescript silver sedan, a typical rental car. Through the tinted glass, Caro's face was barely visible. She hadn't seen me yet. She gripped the steering wheel and stared straight ahead for several seconds. I half expected her to start the engine and back out of the spot, but she didn't. The Caro I remembered had more guts than that.

The car door opened, and I held my breath.

She emerged from the car like a mermaid from the depths of the sea. I'd been stunned by her beauty the first time I'd seen her at the skating facility handing out rental skates in the office. Despite the fact that I'd owned an expensive pair of hockey skates, I approached her under the guise that I wanted to rent skates. The second I looked into her deep blue eyes, I was drawn to her like a magnet to metal. I wanted her, and when I wanted something, I went after it.

She glanced quickly away from me and rummaged through the skates, looking for my size.

"I don't see your size here." She was all businesslike as she returned to the *counter. "You have large feet, and we don't get much call for your size in rental skates."*

I grinned and pounced. "You do know what big feet are an indication of?"

She blushed but had the guts to look me directly in the eyes. "I do, but I haven't seen that theory proven yet." She purposely looked me up and down, pausing briefly at the ever-growing bulge in my crotch.

"I'd be glad to prove it. What time do you get off work?"

"Nine, but you're going to have to work a lot harder than unproven claims regarding big feet to get a date with me."

"Who said I was asking you on a date?" I moved in close to her, leaning across the counter until our lips were inches apart. She didn't shy away but held

her ground and licked those luscious red lips. The girl was toying with me, which drove my teenage hormones into overdrive.

"I do, Mr. Bigfeet." She batted her eyelashes in mock innocence, and I laughed heartily.

"Caro, get back to work!" shouted a woman who'd just walked into the office.

Caro jumped backward as did I, both looking guilty as charged. "Sorry," she mumbled.

I shifted awkwardly from one foot to the other, not wanting to leave, but under the intense scrutiny of Caro's tight-ass boss. "I, uh, okay." I backed away from the counter.

"See you at nine." Caro winked at me.

I broke into a grin and backed into a rack of skate repair and maintenance items. I grabbed for the wire rack, managing to hold it upright. Turning, I ran for the safety of the door with Caro's soft giggle following me.

After that evening, we were together every chance we got. I didn't score that night, and she did make me work for it, but the wait had been more than worth it.

And now this object of my teenage fantasies come reality stood before me. No longer a girl but a woman and a mother and most likely a wife. Despite the situation, my body knew what it wanted, but my body wasn't always a good judge of what was best for me.

I was on guard, as my emotions warred with each other. Anticipation. Resentment. Betrayal. Anger. Hope. Revenge. All of it. Caro had some explaining to do.

She stopped in front of her car and glanced around. When she spotted me, she squared her shoulders and advanced, like a brave warrior marching into battle.

I wouldn't make this easy on her. She'd done the unthinkable in my book. She'd kept my child a secret from me. A guy didn't forget or forgive such a betrayal easily.

"Easton." Her voice was calm and cool, as if our meeting were nothing more than a minor business transaction. I steeled myself against the conflict raging inside me and presented my best poker face, the very one I used when the veterans were giving me shit on and off the ice.

"Caro." I was relieved my own voice was as cool and unemotional as hers.

She started to sit across from me, and I whipped off my coat. "It's wet. Sit on this."

She hesitated, caught off guard by my chivalry, then reached for the coat. For the briefest of moments our fingers touched. Old feelings and memories slammed into me with the force of a head-on collision. And for me, that collision was a near fatality.

I remembered too much. The feel of her soft skin sliding across mine. The little moans she made when I pushed inside her. The way she looked at me as if I were the only man on earth.

Oh, God. Fuck. Damn it to hell.

She was not that girl anymore, and I wasn't that boy. Nothing would ever be the same between us. We'd had puppy love. My memories were clouded by a false perception. The dream was likely far better than the reality.

Unfortunately, that reality looked pretty damn fucking good to me.

But I was wrong. She was deceptive, a schemer. She wanted something from me, but I wanted something in exchange. I had to keep my end goal in mind.

She sat opposite me and stared at her hands clasped in front of her on the table. I waited for her to speak, not giving her the benefit of breaking the ice first.

"Easton," she croaked and cleared her throat. She swallowed, still staring downward, not meeting my gaze. She was nervous. I saw the slight tremor in her hands. Her composure had been an act. Only a bastard would enjoy her discomfort, and I guess at this point in time, I was a bastard.

"I have— You have twins. A boy and a girl."

My smug smile fell off my face, and I shed my composure faster than a stripper sheds her clothes. "How do you know they're mine?" I heard my husky, tense voice and hardly recognized it.

"DNA." She didn't explain further, and I didn't ask, but there was a question of how she would've gotten my DNA to test.

"I'll want to do my own test."

"We can do that."

"Why are you coming to me now? Why tell me at all since you obviously planned on keeping their father a secret from them indefinitely?"

She cringed and met my angry gaze. "I'm sorry. I didn't know."

"You didn't know?" My voice rose until I was almost shouting. My patience had developed a short fuse around her. A couple walking a dog stared in our direction and slowed their pace. I lowered my voice, not wanting to alarm them enough they intervened or called the police. "How could you not know?"

"It's complicated." She wrung her hands over and over. "When you left me, I didn't know I was pregnant. My former boyfriend was there to pick up the pieces, and I slept with him, trying to ease the pain. I assumed they were his. When I found out I was pregnant, he insisted on marrying me."

"I see." I didn't see. Regardless, some other man had raised my children as his. They had to be six years old by my calculations.

"I'm sorry. I would've told you sooner if I'd known."

"You're sorry? That's all you can say is you're sorry? You don't think a father has the right to know his children? You don't think I have a say in their lives? Fuck you." Anger rolled through me, blotting out the pain and giving me strength to get through this. I embraced my fury, wallowing in it, welcoming the way it wiped out all rational thinking. I didn't want to be rational right now. I wanted to shout about the injustice. I wanted to blame her, make her feel the guilt of denying me the right to what was mine. My children. Two of them. My blood. A boy and a girl.

She stood. "I understand why you're upset, but getting mad at me isn't going to fix the situation. You have my number. I'll be in town for a few more days. Call me when you're ready to talk."

"I'm ready now." I stood, too, and stalked after her as she walked purposefully to her car. "We're not done yet," I growled, knowing I sounded threatening but not caring.

"Miss? Are you okay?" The older couple walking the dog had circled back around and stood near her car.

"I'm fine. Thank you." She offered them a sweet smile. I stopped in my tracks as they stepped in front of me, preventing me from following her.

"I'm so sorry." Tears flowed down Caro's face. Her eyes pleaded with me to forgive her. My feet were anchored to the sidewalk. Before I regained my composure, she got in her car and tore out of the parking lot.

This was the second time she'd run out on me.

Chapter Eight

TATTERED COURAGE

--Caroline--

I was shaking so badly I could barely drive. Glancing in my rearview mirror, I didn't see any cars behind me. I pulled down a side street and into an alley. After shutting off the car, I lay my head on the steering wheel and gulped in great lungfuls of air.

I had to stay strong. I had to get ahold of myself.

I didn't know what kind of reception I'd expected from Easton, but I'd hoped for a better one than what I'd gotten. He was justifiably angry, and he'd gotten angrier and angrier, much like his daughter had a tendency to do.

His daughter.

Oh, my God. What had I done?

Heaven help me. I deserved to rot in hell. Or worse, I deserved whatever the future might bring. Why hadn't I done the math all those years ago and realized the twins could be his? We'd always been so careful, and I was on the pill. It'd never occurred to me they were anything other than Mark's kids. That sounded ignorant of me, and I understood why Easton thought I was full of shit.

I'd deluded myself into believing he wouldn't want to be a father any more than he'd wanted to be with me once that summer had ended.

I'd seen it in his eyes. He wasn't going to walk away. He wasn't going to be an uninvolved father. No one could be that angry if they didn't want a relationship with their children.

He wanted to know his kids.

I'd opened Pandora's box.

I'd let this man back into my life and into my kids' lives.

I was the worst kind of fool to think he meant nothing to me. He did, he always had, and he always would. One look at him, and I was ready to fall into bed with him. Even worse, fall for him.

How would the kids react when they found out they had another father? It didn't matter that I hadn't known until recently, they'd blame me, because they were angry at the world for taking Mark from them.

I deserved their anger. I deserved Easton's anger.

How had I not figured this out sooner?

I was a horrible person, and soon everyone would know it.

Wiping my face on my sleeve, I called Fran.

"How did it go?" she asked before even saying hello.

"He hates me. He's livid." I'd thought I was done crying, but I wasn't. The sobs came unbidden from somewhere so deep inside me they were physically painful.

"He'll calm down. This has to come as a shock to him."

"He was so angry, a concerned couple intervened. I got the hell out of there."

"You ran away from him again?" I heard the chastising tone in Fran's voice.

"Yes," I sniffled. I was such a sniveling idiot.

"You have to stop doing that. Running isn't getting you anywhere. It's only prolonging the agony. Rip off the bandage and get on with it."

"I think he's going to want a relationship with the kids."

"And that's a bad thing?"

"It could be. How are they going to feel about this? About me?"

"They'll be angry, but they already are angry. You'll get beyond this and be stronger for it."

I fished a tissue from my purse and blew my nose in a very unladylike way. I sounded like the Canadian geese that hung around by the lake back home every night.

"How long ago did you leave him?"

"Several minutes."

"Go back there. Now."

I shook my head, even though she couldn't see me. "Not yet. He needs time to cool off."

"Perhaps, but you need to finish what you started instead of scampering away like a scared rabbit."

"I know," I admitted with resignation. "Just not now."

"Then when? Do you really think he won't get angry again tomorrow or next week or next month? Tell him everything, then he can get angry and get over it one final time, but doling it out a little at a time isn't doing either of you any favors."

Fran was right, of course.

"Okay, wish me luck."

"Good luck, honey. Everything will be fine. You must have faith."

I gathered my tattered courage, started the car, and backed carefully out of the alley.

--Easton--

I didn't need this shit. She'd run out on me again.

What the fuck?

Instead of leaving, I walked along the shoreline in an attempt to get my head on straight and calm myself down. If I drove home now, I'd have a major case of road rage, and I wouldn't unleash that anger on anyone.

And I was angry, but I worked to rein in my previously nonexistent temper.

The couple who'd intervened had left finally after sticking around long enough to make sure I didn't follow Caro.

I was the guy who never showed anger, but this situation went beyond what I seemed able to control, yet control it I must. I had so many questions, and she was the only one with the answers. I was ashamed of losing it, but I doubted anyone would be much better under my circumstances.

I was considerably calmer when I returned to my truck and sat behind the steering wheel. I was about to start the engine when that same rental car turned slowly into the parking lot.

She'd come back.

I didn't get out. I waited for her to make the first move.

She walked the short distance to my car and opened the passenger-side door. In my peripheral vision, one shapely leg in skinny jeans followed the other. I swallowed hard and gripped the steering wheel. Next came her delectable ass, which she sat on my leather seat.

Enough already.

I was torturing myself. I kept my eyes straight ahead. Looking at her made me both angry and horny, along with resentful and needy. None of which would help my current situation.

"I'm sorry," she said quietly as she shut the door.

"I know," I said in a voice colder than the frigid air outside this car.

She dug in her purse, which was almost as big as my hockey duffle. My mother had carried a ginormous purse like that when we were younger.

"I meant to give this to you earlier before I lost my nerve." She held out a manila envelope. Frowning, I took it from her, careful not to touch her fingers, and opened it. I pulled out the contents, which consisted of a handful of photographs. She could've given me her cell phone to scroll through the images, but instead, she'd had photographs printed. For some reason, the gesture melted my frozen heart a bit. At least, it was an olive branch, and I would graciously accept it as such.

I stared at the first photo of two children smiling for the camera. The little girl was dressed in a pink frilly dress, her blonde hair and blue eyes reminding me of her mother. Yet there was something in the stubborn set of her jaw and mischief shining in those eyes that reminded me of myself. The little boy had brown eyes and dark brown hair. He wore a sweatshirt and jeans. He was barely smiling, his gaze intense. He was the spitting image of me. My heart soared as I gaped at the two of them.

I was a father. A fucking father. They were part of me, and I was part of them. My chest swelled with pride for these two little lives I'd helped create. They were my blood, and I knew in that instant I'd fight to be a part of their lives.

"That's Hailey and Heath," Caro said.

I didn't comment but turned to the next photograph. Heath was in full hockey gear and racing down the ice. Emotion surged inside me, filling my chest with a mixture of wonder, sorrow, and love. He was my son. I couldn't speak, and I kept my gaze turned away from Caro. Hot tears burned in my eyes, and my heart felt as if it might burst from my chest.

My son.

The next picture was of Hailey, also on skates, but in a figure-staking costume and executing a spin. A vise closed over my chest, and I rubbed my eyes with my fists. She was my daughter as much as he was my son.

Holy fuck.

I'd been slammed against the boards headfirst. I'd never known such pain yet such incredible awe for these children I'd helped put on this earth.

"They're athletic, like you. Heath is the best player on his team. Hailey is a star among her group." Caro's voice was husky, betraying her own misgivings and regrets. This hadn't been easy for her either. I almost felt sorry for her.

I said nothing, merely looked through the three pictures again. There were no words when a man found out he was a father for the first time. No words to explain the emotions filling my heart with joy for the future and sadness for all I'd missed.

I cleared my throat and held the photographs tenderly in my fingers. Finally, I lifted my head and met Caro's gaze. Her eyes were full of sympathy, laden with guilt, and sprinkled with apprehension.

"What do you want from me?" I croaked huskily, just grateful I didn't break down and sob and reveal weakness to her. I revealed weakness to no one.

When my dad died, the pain of my loss overwhelmed me. I never wanted to feel pain like that again, and I'd managed to keep my emotions in check until I'd met Caro that summer. I'd let her in, I'd become immersed in her, and I'd walked away when the summer ended.

I met her gaze, displaying my hockey face, the one that betrayed no emotion other than determination. She stared at her hands in her lap. I waited, calling forth patience. She sighed and lifted her gaze to meet mine.

"My husband, Mark, died a few months ago, and my in-laws admitted he'd been adopted. They encouraged me to get DNA tests done on the twins so they'd know their genetic and health backgrounds. I did, and I never expected the results. Never. I promise."

"You didn't do the math and figure it out?"

"No, I never...I never even considered... You have to believe me." She wrung her hands again, and I recalled she was quite the hand wringer whenever she was nervous, like the night I broke up with her.

"I don't *have* to do shit." Her possible intentions slapped me in the face. She wasn't here because she was righting a wrong. She was here for money because she was desperate. I'd be a fool if I didn't demand an official DNA test, even though I already knew the results.

"You want money?" I didn't exactly mean to sound as accusatory as I did, but it came out that way, and I ran with it.

She lifted her head with pride and met my gaze with sheer determination. "No, that's not why I'm here. Mark had a modest life insurance policy. I plan on going to school to get my LPN."

"How modest?"

"I don't see where that's any of your concern. I'm here because it was the right thing to do. That's all. I don't want your fucking money."

"They're my children, and my responsibility, too," I said, testing the sound of the words on my tongue.

"I'm not here because I want money. I'm really not."

I didn't believe her. The timing was too coincidental. I shot her a glare.

"I don't want you to feel obligated," she said.

"They're my children. They *are* my obligation." I turned to face her, wanting to make myself perfectly clear. "I also fully intend to exercise my parental rights."

Her eyes grew big and she went back to hand wringing. "In what way?" Her voice held a hint of steel I hadn't heard before. I'd stirred up Mama Bear.

"I want all the rights granted to me by law. My attorney will contact your attorney. Give me the information."

"I don't have an attorney."

"Then he'll contact you to work out the legal paperwork and details. I'm sure he'll demand an official DNA test also, but I've seen enough. I know they're mine."

"Paperwork? Is that necessary?"

"Hell yeah. I don't want you disappearing when you feel like it. No fucking way. I'm their father, and I'm fucking going to be their father." My hold on my temper was slipping, and I fought to control my irritation.

"No, I won't disappear on you. I promise."

"Right, like you haven't the last two times we met?" I rolled my eyes contemptuously, annoyed I was behaving like a spoiled child but doing it anyway. "When can I meet them?"

"I...uh...I don't know. I'd prefer we not go there right now."

"Are you fucking nuts? They're my children, and I have rights."

"Do your rights override what's best for the children?"

I sobered slightly, considering her words. "Isn't knowing their father best for them?"

"They had a father. A good one. They don't need another, especially one who drinks until he passes out and sleeps with random women."

Her words stung, but I couldn't deny I'd done my fair share of being a bad boy since I'd made the pros. "I want to know them."

"In time. You have to prove to me you're serious about being in their lives, not just when it's convenient, but especially when it isn't. I don't trust you or your ability to put others before yourself."

She had a point, but I hated to concede that fact.

"They're still grieving over the loss of their father. Maybe it'd be better if they got to know you as a friend first. They've had a tough time of it."

"You want me to deceive them?"

"Not exactly. I need to be sure you're going to stick around. That you won't get tired of them like you got tired of me."

"I won't." I bristled, ready to chew her ass, but some still-remorseful part of me recognized the truth of her words. She didn't know me. All she knew was how much I'd been partying lately. She had no idea what kind of person I was or how my presence might affect her children. I'd be cautious if I were in her position; any caring parent would. That didn't mean I wasn't pissed as hell at the situation. I was.

"I need to see your commitment to them before I let you in their life as their father. Throwing money at them when you have a lot to throw around is easy. Being a real father is the hard part."

I clenched my fists and counted to ten. I had to maintain a level of civility with her. Having parents at each other's throats wouldn't do anyone any good. "Okay, you want to see commitment? I'm moving you to Seattle. I'll have the arrangements made. I leave for a road trip in a few days. By the time we get back, it'll all be settled. I'll get my people to manage the details."

"I am not moving to Seattle."

"Like fuck you aren't. What's keeping you wherever you are?" My jaw hardened, and she drew back at the restrained fury on my face. I looked away for several seconds. When I turned back, my face was a careful mask of indifference.

She stared out the windshield as if thinking long and hard. When she turned back to me, her defiance had turned to defeat. "We'll move here. They have a right to know you, same as you have a right to know them. You can be an old family friend, and we've reconnected. I require I be there whenever you're with them."

"Have it your way."

"Thank you."

Caro scratched out her personal deets such as snail mail on a piece of paper and handed it to me. She reached for the door handle, ready to bolt at any moment. "Is that all?"

I guessed it was for now. I had a game to play tonight, and playing hockey was currently the furthest thing from my mind.

"Yeah, I'll be in contact. I have a game tonight but have tomorrow off. I'll call you to set up something. You'll also be hearing from my attorney."

She frowned, opened the door, and beat a hasty retreat to her car. I watched her get in and drive away. Only then did I wonder what I'd gotten myself into, not with the kids but with her.

Chapter Nine

BAD GAME

--Easton--

The Sockeyes' home arena was electric as we marched as a team in a line through the tunnel and out the arena gate onto the ice for our pregame warm-ups. I put one foot on the slick surface, ready to skate energetically around the boards. Instead, my skate stuck to the ice as if it'd been covered in glue. My ass hit the ice first with my legs and arms flapping.

The good-sized crowd in attendance to see warm-ups cheered at my misfortune. Playing the good sport, I scrambled to my feet, pulled off the skate guards I'd forgotten about, and did a low bow to the fans. They loved it, but their appreciation of my good humor did nothing to assuage the burning embarrassment. Of course, the jerk in the media booth chose to replay the scene on the large center screens.

Face flaming, I skated to middle ice, where some teammates were doing drills.

"Nice one, rookie." Cedric slapped me on the back so hard I almost went down again, which brought guffaws from the team veterans and my now former friends.

I tried to concentrate on my drills and my skating, but my brain would not engage. Not only was I obsessing over my fall, but I was obsessing over being a father and, even worse, over Caro. By the time I got back from tomorrow's road trip in a week, she'd be moved to Seattle.

I'd solved Caro's living situation earlier that afternoon. The team's goalie coach had been living in a condo courtesy of the team owner until he'd bought a house and moved into it about a month ago. It was dumb luck that the place had come available at the same time I'd asked Mina, Ethan Parker's scary-assed assistant, if she knew of any openings in the Parker Union Condo Building.

I'd wanted to pay the rent. Ethan insisted on not taking any rent. He said I'd be doing him a favor as he'd write off the loss of income from the unit.

I didn't believe a write-off was that big of a favor, but I graciously accepted. NHL rookies made a good salary, but lots of rookies spent way above their means in a short amount of time. I didn't want to be one of them. Kaden was already heading that way, despite lectures from Steele and me about the virtues of saving for a rainy day. By and large, most hockey careers were short-lived, allowing us a small portion of our lives to earn the big bucks. A guy never knew when he'd suffer a game-ending injury or when the league no longer wanted his services.

Now that I had kids to think about, being careful with my money and investing wisely were more crucial than ever.

I was a father.

I'd been repeating those four words over and over all day, still not used to the sound of them. I vowed to be the best dad a guy could be. I hadn't told anyone but my roommates yet, and they'd surprisingly kept their mouths shut. I'd eventually tell the entire team and my family, but right now I wanted time to adjust without others' well-meaning interference.

My night went from bad to worse. I wasn't doing anything right, as my skates had a mind of their own, my stick missed every pass, and my head wasn't in the game.

I was fucking mad at myself. I trudged to the locker room and hung my head. The guys left me alone, allowing me to work out my bad game for myself. I'd had bad games before, and I'd risen above them. They happened to all of us. We were human after all.

And now I was moving Caro across the hall from me. I'd be lying if I pretended her presence wouldn't have an effect on me. We had chemistry, and from the few times I'd been around her, that chemistry was as strong as ever.

I wasn't looking for a relationship, and starting one up again with her would only cause problems when it ended. I had to maintain a polite and friendly distance for our children's sakes. No options.

--Caroline--

I checked out and hurried to the airport as soon as Easton and I finished our talk this morning. I'd managed to snag a flight to Chicago at noon and was home before the first puck drop of the Sockeyes game.

Once I'd arrived home and collected the kids from their grandparents, I'd called my best friend, Juniper. While Fran and Howard were supportive and understanding, I needed someone who'd known me all my life and called me on my bullshit when I needed it. I'd met Juniper in first grade, and we'd been friends through high school. In fact, she'd been around that summer and met Easton and dated a few of his teammates. Juniper was coming off a bad divorce to a lazy, abusive asshole and needed me as much as I needed her.

She loved hockey, so it was a no-brainer that we'd end up watching the game.

Easton played like a man who'd just found out he was the father to a set of six-year-old twins, including his ass-plant on the ice, which was replayed over and over again throughout the game. I felt responsible for his crappy game. Nothing was going right for him tonight. I worried our presence might endanger his spot on the team, because I worried about everything.

"He's playing like crap," Juniper noted as Easton tripped over his own feet and passed the puck to an opposing player, who sailed down the ice and scored a goal.

"It's not one of his better games, I'd guess."

"You aren't blaming yourself, are you?" Juniper said, picking up on my misery.

"Sorta."

"He's a professional. You're not responsible for how he plays. He needs to put on his big-boy boxers and not let his personal life interfere with his game. And his graceful entrance on the ice was a classic. He'll be living that one down forever." Junie laughed her ass off, not caring about Easton's bruised ego.

"It was funny," I admitted. "And you're right, I'm not responsible for his on-ice performances."

"I'm always right."

We'd ordered out for pizza, and I'd almost gotten a smile out of Heath when I told him he could stay up and watch the hockey game since it wasn't a school night. The Blackhawks were his team, and they happened to be playing the Sockeyes. Hailey forgot she was mad at me and snuggled up next to me with Rusty purring on her lap. Rusty was my old tabby. I'd had him since I'd been fourteen. He'd been with me through so much good and bad in my life.

"Who are you talking about?" asked Heath from between us.

I met Juniper's eyes over Heath's head. She shrugged and left it up to me to explain.

"No one you'd know," I said, taking the easy way out. It was intermission, and they were showing the salmon being tossed back and forth in Pike Place Market.

"Can we go to Seattle and throw fish?" Heath asked.

Maybe there was a God, because my son just gave me a segue.

"Sure, we can do that. What would you think about moving to Seattle?"

"And leave Nana and Grandpa?" Hailey stuck out her lower lip and shook her head. "I don't want to move."

Heath didn't say anything.

"If we move to Seattle, we can eventually get that dog you've been wanting." Bribery wasn't beneath me.

"We can?" Hailey perked up and was all smiles for a moment. Then her frown made a reappearance. "What about Nana and Grandpa?"

"They're moving somewhere warmer, honey, so they aren't going to be living here either. They'll come visit."

"Okay," she said, somewhat mollified.

"If we move to Seattle, I can throw fish?" Heath had a one-track mind, and his pleasures in life revolved around hockey. So much like his father.

"Yes, you can."

"When can we move?" Heath nodded vigorously. This was the most enthusiasm I'd seen from him other than when he was playing hockey since his father had died. He even smiled at me. I wasn't naïve enough to think we'd gotten over that hump permanently, but we'd turned a corner. Tomorrow, he'd probably be back to sullen and angry, but hopefully, those moments would become less and less.

Hailey watched us, quiet for once, and yawned. "Hockey is boring."

"You can go to bed."

"No, I'm fine."

Things were looking up. They were behaving like my children once more.

An hour later, I put both of them to bed.

Juniper was waiting for me when I returned.

"When were you going to tell me you were moving to Seattle?" The hurt on her face was obvious as she rose from the couch to pour herself a glass of wine.

I followed her to the kitchen and accepted the glass she held out to me. I slid onto the counter stool and regarded her. "I'm sorry. I didn't have a chance to tell you."

"I've always wanted to live in Seattle," she said wistfully.

A crazy notion struck me, and I jumped on it before my analytical side counted off all the reasons my idea wasn't a good one.

"Why don't you go with us?"

Juniper frowned, her brow furrowing as she considered my offer. "Is there room where you're staying? I mean, I don't need much room, and I don't mind sleeping on the couch. My job is dead-end, boring crap, so walking away wouldn't break my heart."

"It'd be an adventure," said the least-adventurous person in this room, but I was gathering steam. If Juniper came with me, I wouldn't feel so lost and alone. We could both use a fresh start away from the ghosts of our pasts and our dysfunctional families.

"I'm going to do it. You're sure I won't be an inconvenience?"

"I'm positive."

We hugged each other and spent the remainder of the evening planning our escape to the great Pacific Northwest. By the time she left, I felt much better about the move.

I settled on the couch as a rare, blissful quiet surrounded me.

I was doing the right thing by starting fresh elsewhere. Well, maybe not totally fresh, since Easton was baggage from my teenage years.

My biggest problem would be resisting him, knowing he blamed me for missing the first six years of the twins' lives. Seeing him brought back a flood of memories of some of the happiest moments in my life that didn't involve my children. I refused to fall prey to the sorrow of knowing we'd never get a second chance. I didn't need a second chance. I didn't need a man in my life. I needed to get my nursing degree, get my career on track, and learn to live on my own two feet and not depend on others.

If Easton insisted on supporting his children, I'd accept his offer, but the last thing I wanted was to be dependent on any man indefinitely. Once I had my nursing career underway, I'd put any spare child support in trust or something for the kids' college funds. I wouldn't use a penny of it.

I had my pride, and I'd someday soon have the luxury of indulging in a few prideful moments.

I closed my eyes, letting peace wash over me for the first time in months. I was doing the right thing for myself, for Easton, and most of all, for Hailey and Heath.

· · ·

I was lying in a field on a blanket looking up at the millions of stars in the sky. Easton lay next to me, his hands behind his head. In one week, his summer hockey program would be over, and he'd be leaving. We hadn't talked about that particular elephant in the room. Both of us avoided the subject, and I didn't want to be the first to broach the obvious.

Easton must've sensed me staring at him. He rolled over onto his side and propped his head up with an elbow. He reached for a lock of my hair with his free hand and turned it around his finger.

His dark eyes settled on mine. Every time he looked at me like that, my body came alive with an intense, driving need I had very little control over. I expected him to pull me into his arms and begin the initial stages of foreplay, followed by passionate fucking. That had been our normal MO for the past couple months.

This time, he surprised me. He appeared to be in a rare introspective mood. Easton was a doer, not a thinker. He lived by actions, not so much by words, while I was a planner and a worrier.

"Caro, I'm leaving in a week."

There, he'd finally addressed the elephant.

"I know."

"I've never really known what love is, except for the love of my family, but if I could love somebody, it'd be you."

My heart soared with joy. Even though his hadn't been an admission of love, I'd take it as such. I was a teenage girl, and I wore my emotions on my sleeve.

"I feel the same way." I didn't know what love was either, and I didn't have the advantage of experiencing the love of a family like he had. In fact, my mother considered me an inconvenience, and my father barely knew I existed.

"I want us to enjoy this last week together and not worry about the future. I know you. You're already fretting about it."

I had to smile, and he smiled back, one of his smiles that made me all gooey and giddy inside. That same smile that made me drop my panties every single time he aimed the full force of it at me. This time wasn't an exception. We couldn't keep our hands off each other, and in seconds we were naked and fucking each other into mind-blowing orgasms.

The world ceased to exist outside of the two of us and this star-filled night.

--Easton--

*M*y teammates talked me into going out with them after the game. I wasn't in the mood to party, but I wasn't exactly in the mood to sit at home and lick my wounded ego either.

At least we were at a bar with a private back room rather than a loud nightclub. I definitely wasn't in the mood for clubbing, but a few beers and a pizza wouldn't be so bad. Beer might dull the ache in my chest at least for a little while, and talking hockey might distract me.

I took a chair at a long table and poured a beer from one of the many pitchers. Teammates drank and laughed around me. Some played pool; others hung in groups with and without their WAGs. Many of us were stag, like me.

Ice tapped Kaden on the shoulder and motioned for him to vacate the chair next to me. "Get your ass out of my chair, rookie."

Kaden whipped around, ready to rip the asshole a new one. The look on his face was priceless when he realized that *asshole* was our team captain, the last guy on our team we had any interest in messing with. He scrambled out of his chair, almost tipping it over, and made a hasty retreat.

Ice claimed the recently vacated seat and sucked down water from many of the glasses placed on the table by our conscientious waitress. I'd never seen Ice drink anything with alcohol in it and had heard he was a recovering alcoholic. I didn't know, and I wasn't asking.

I avoided his gaze, wishing he'd go away and leave me alone. I didn't know why he'd taken me on as his personal project. While I was flattered, I preferred flying under the radar right now.

In practice, he always made a point of skating with me, forcing me to go up against the best defenseman in the league. My game was steadily improving, even with tonight's setback. Playing against Ice either improved a guy or broke him. I was proud to say I hadn't broken, only become stronger.

"What the fuck happened to you tonight, rook?" Ice demanded, not holding back. He tapped on his glass with a fork for emphasis.

"Bad game. We all have them," I muttered defensively and slouched down into my chair. I crossed my arms over my chest and glowered stubbornly, refusing to look our fearless leader in the eye.

He was quiet for a long time. Ice wasn't one to waste words, which was why we listened when he spoke. Regardless, his silence disconcerted me. I chanced a glance his direction. He was rubbing his chin and studying me thoughtfully.

"Yeah, well, I guess you were due for an off night," he conceded, much to my surprise. He waved his hand at the waitress. "Can I get a Coke, a chicken Caesar, and a T-bone, medium-rare? Oh, and add shrimp and a baked potato, everything on it. The rookie here is paying tonight. Put it on his bill." He pointed at me with a rare twinkle in his eyes.

The waitress nodded and cast a sultry smile in my direction. I ignored her and hunkered down in my chair. I wasn't in the mood for flirting.

"Hey, guys, did you hear that?" Cedric shouted gleefully, getting everyone's attention. "Big E, here, is treating us tonight. Eat up and enjoy!"

Cheers went around the table. I sighed. I'd known my time was coming. Kaden and Steele had already covered a couple bills. My turn. Next year we'd have our shot at torturing the next group of rookies.

Cedric and Rush raised their hands to get the waitress's attention and ordered steak and the best Scotch in the house. I rolled my eyes, even as I was resigned to my fate.

When I turned my attention back to Ice, he was scrutinizing me with one of his patented intense expressions.

"How's Avery doing? I notice she's not here tonight," I asked, hoping to shift the subject away from my bad night. Ice's wife was a horse trainer and a really nice, down-to-earth person. She was also my cousin Coop's sister-in-law. He was married to her sister.

Ice looked around and lowered his voice. "Can you keep a secret?"

"Yes." I hid my astonishment that he was confiding in a lowly rookie.

"She's pregnant. Only a few people know. We're not ready to announce it yet. Anyway, she isn't feeling too good tonight."

"Wow, dude, that's cool. The baby on the way, that is." I hoped he didn't notice the odd tone in my voice. Seven years ago, I would've been the one announcing to my teammates that I was having twins. I frowned, unable to visualize how such an announcement would go down among my teenage hockey-playing cohorts. They'd have either congratulated me or told me to pray for my sanity while kissing any chance at an NHL career goodbye.

Maybe things had worked out for the best in the long run. The odds would've been stacked against me when it came to having a successful professional hockey career while supporting twins and a wife. Hell, I'd had two years left in high school. Most likely, I would've been forced to quit hockey, and possibly high school, and gone to work at the local grocery store or something, and our marriage would've failed within the year if I'd married Caro.

Ice beamed at me, and he rarely beamed at anyone. "Yeah. Our first. Pretty damn excited about it."

"I can imagine." He had no idea. "Congratulations, man."

"Thanks. Being a dad is probably going to be the toughest and most rewarding thing I've ever done."

"Yeah, I'm sure it is." I wasn't being patronizing. I believed what he was saying based on my short experience being a father.

He winked at me. "Later." Ice stood and walked over to Cedric and Rush, leaving me alone with my own thoughts regarding parenthood.

I was a father.

I had to behave like one and set a good example. I had two little lives depending on me. Looking up to me. Maybe even idolizing me. A thrilling yet scary thought. I'd idolized my firefighter father. He'd walked on water and was invincible in my eyes until that fateful night when he'd gone into a burning apartment building to rescue a baby. He'd handed the baby out the window to a waiting firefighter just before the roof caved in on him. He'd died a hero, but he'd left a heart-broken mother and three children behind. God willing, I'd always be there for my kids.

What kind of father would I be compared to mine? I'd been ten when he'd died. He'd played junior hockey but never been good enough for the big leagues. My mom had played college hockey, so my brothers and I came by our talent naturally. I recall my dad being gone a lot, but he'd devoted time to us whenever he was home. Juggling firefighting and fatherhood had to be a challenge, just like juggling hockey and fatherhood.

Losing my father at ten had made a lasting impression on me, prob-ably in more ways than I realized. Kids had a tendency to blame them-selves no matter how crazy that might be. For a long time, I wondered if there was something I could've done to make him stay home that day. He'd covered a shift for another guy. He wasn't supposed to be working. I'd learned early in life the mortality of those you loved, and I'd avoided close relationships from that point on other than my family. Yeah, I'd had the same college girlfriend for three years, but we'd stayed together out of convenience, not necessarily a deep, burning need for each other. I'd needed Caro way more, despite our short time together.

My mom had never remarried, never been interested in another relationship. She often declared that my father had been the love of her life. She'd been lucky enough to find a good man once, and she wasn't messing with her perfect record.

What effects would losing Mark have on my kids long term? Did they feel guilt like I did and blame themselves or even their mother? Was there anything Caro and I could do to help them through it? I truly had no fucking idea. I was ill-equipped for fatherhood.

I scanned the crowd and found Brick. He'd found out a few years ago he was a father to a little girl. Brick had been the ultimate party boy until Macy appeared on his doorstop—literally. She was a figure skater too. He doted on her and was constantly showing anyone he cornered countless pictures of her.

I wondered if picking his brain would make him suspicious, or maybe I should tell him the truth? I didn't plan on keeping my fatherhood a secret, but I hadn't figured out when or how to tell the rest of my teammates, friends, and family.

Shoving my chair away from the table, I walked over to where Brick sat with several of the veterans. I wedged a chair between him and Matt LaRue, who was also a dad to two boys. Maybe they'd both impart some advice to a new father.

They shot daggers at me. I was a rookie, after all, pushing my way into their conversation. Not normal or accepted rookie behavior, but I'd never been a rule follower or even cared about shit like that.

"What the fuck, rookie?" Brick growled, while Matt said nothing but cocked his head to indicate interest.

"Sorry, but I need some advice." I lowered my voice so only they could hear, though I did notice team gossip Ziggy leaning across the table to eavesdrop. If you wanted anything spread to every member of the team, he was your go-to guy. He loved to be in on everything and the guy in the know.

I glowered at him with a silent mind-your-own-business warning, and he smirked at me. Ziggy wasn't easily intimidated, but that held true of just about everyone on the team, or we wouldn't be professional hockey players.

"Advice? Take off your skate guards before getting on the ice," Brick said and elbowed Matt.

"Don't put your helmet on backward," Matt laughed. The two of them fist-bumped as if they were fucking comedians. I rolled my eyes.

"Fuck you both. Funny. Really funny. I don't need hockey advice."

"You sure as fuck needed it tonight," Brick pointed out, and I cringed. The goalie didn't seem to care he'd dealt a near knockout blow. Hockey players were harsh like that. Either develop a thick skin or get out of the game.

I shot him a glare before continuing. "I need dad advice."

Their smirks slid off their faces in record time, and they gaped at me in open-mouthed disbelief. I'd delivered the ultimate sucker punch. They hadn't seen that coming.

"Dad advice?" Matt recovered first, shaking his head as if to clear it.

"What kind of dad advice?" Brick choked on the word.

"I found out a few days ago I'm a father to six-year-old twins."

Brick jerked back in his seat like he'd been slapped. Matt furrowed his brow and continued to stare at me with confusion. I glanced at Ziggy, who was all ears, his eyes as wide as pucks. Great. Within an hour, the team crier would notify the entire team. I ignored him. I didn't have any other choice.

I dived into the story, telling them what I knew. Brick and Matt listened intently, along with Ziggy and our backup goalie, Jacques, a.k.a. Jock, who'd joined the conversation. Jock had five kids, so he knew a little something about parenting too.

After I finished, the table was silent as my teammates digested the information I'd given them.

"Part of me is unreasonably angry at the mother for the time I missed with my kids."

Brick nodded sympathetically. His own daughter had been dumped on his doorstep at five years old. He'd had no prior knowledge of her. "I understand that. I was angry as fuck regarding the time I'd missed, too, but you have to let it go. That anger will eat you up inside, and in your case, she didn't know. You need to believe what she told you."

"Forgive and move on. The kids need both of you to present a united front for their sakes. It's all about the kids now, not about your hurt feelings or time lost. Concentrate on making up that time and being the best father you can be," Matt added.

"Make sure everything you do is for the betterment of your kids. Selfishness has zero place in a father's heart," added Jock.

"She doesn't want them to know I'm their father yet."

"I can't blame her," Ice spoke up from behind me. "She's gun-shy, and she's going to protect her kids. You can't be mad about that."

Oh, but I was. I was mad at her for so very many things, unreasonably so. I had to get beyond it, but I hadn't reached that point yet.

"We should give Big E a baby shower." Rush sat down across the table. The asshole grinned at me. "We can play party games and watch him open gifts."

The jerks hooted with laughter.

"They better be drinking games," Ziggy added and more hilarity ensued. These guys were idiots.

"I'll give him a box of condoms," Rush said.

"It's a little late for the condoms." Ice snorted and took a chug of his Coke. I was grateful Ice didn't drink. He was enough of a demanding dickhead stone-cold sober.

"Do they have strippers at baby showers?" Kaden waggled his brows and leered at no one in particular.

"She can jump out of a cake in nothing but a diaper," Ziggy said.

"I'm in." Caveman fist-bumped Ziggy, and they both grinned at me.

Who invited all these assholes into my private conversation?

"All right, ladies, dinner's being served!" Cedric interrupted the clowns planning my imaginary shower. The guys scrambled for seats but not before almost every one of them slapped me on the back and congratulated me.

"Dude, I don't think we're getting that stripper," Ziggy said sadly.

"No, buddy, I don't think we are." I sighed and dug into my steak. I might as well join 'em, but I wasn't going to be able to beat 'em or even get a word in.

--Caroline--

Easton didn't waste any time. Once I'd agreed to his plan to move us to Seattle, things happened at an overwhelming speed. By now it was mid-November, and the holidays were looming on the horizon. I wanted to get the kids moved and settled into a new school as quickly as possible to lessen any strain on them.

I was officially overwhelmed. No amount of list making and worrying would organize this colossal life change.

Easton left on a road trip on Tuesday and returned the following Wednesday morning, which happened to be today, one week before Thanksgiving. I was pretty sure he'd want to meet the kids immediately, and I wasn't prepared for that inevitable step just yet.

He'd been true to his word. His attorney contacted me about a temporary parenting plan. The movers had packed up our stuff and moved it to Seattle to be put into storage until we moved into our new home. We'd flown to Seattle over the weekend and were housed in a very nice suite in a hotel near where we'd be living, which I'd yet to see.

I enrolled the kids in school immediately, and on Monday they attended their first day of class. I didn't worry much about Hailey. She was an excellent student, inquisitive and bright. She loved school. Heath, on the other hand, considered going to school a necessary evil and lived for the final bell every day so he could play hockey.

Juniper was with us every step of the way, and I appreciated her more than words would ever say. She'd already found a job at a car dealership processing paperwork. She liked it so far. Benefits were good, and the pay was okay. Neither of us had realized how high the cost of living was in Seattle, though, and a good wage where we'd lived was, in Seattle, closer to living at poverty level.

We were all anxious to get settled into the condo. The four of us in a one-bedroom hotel suite, no matter how nice, was challenging. This move was putting a dent in my depleted bank account, despite Easton paying most of the bills. I was paying for our meals, as the hotel only had a small fridge in the room, and we were eating out daily.

This particular morning, I was fretting about Easton's return, knowing I'd be hearing from him soon. I didn't have to wait long. The text messages started about seven a.m. I read the first few and ignored the rest. Juniper, who didn't work a regular shift, flopped on the couch next to me, still in her pajamas. Her hair was a mess, and she was yawning. "Aren't you going to look at that text?" She glanced at my phone, which had been beeping urgently for a few minutes.

"It's Easton, and he wants to meet this morning. Go over every-thing. The condo will be ready in a few days."

"Then meet with him."

"I'm not ready yet. It's not a good time."

"It'll never be a good time." Juniper rolled her eyes. "Putting off this meeting isn't going to make things easier. You're here and committed to going through with this."

"Regardless, he'll want to meet the kids right away. They're still adjusting to the move, and his appearance might set them back. I need to make a plan, figure out how to handle this for the kids' sakes."

"You've had a week to devise a plan. So far all I've seen is a garbage can full of half-finished lists. Quit worrying. Kids are resilient. They'll bounce back."

"My kids also hold grudges. They've been taking out their grief on me ever since their dad died. When they find out about Easton, they'll be furious. I'm not sure how I'll go about explaining the situation to them. They're only six."

"They might be six, but they're bright kids, and they will forgive you."

"I wish I had your confidence."

"Mom, Heath stole my candy bar!" Hailey ran into the room, tears streaking down her face and sobbing as if she'd lost something far more valuable than a candy bar. Heath stood behind her, saying noth-ing. His face was void of all emotion, reminding me of his father during a hockey game.

"First of all, how did you get a candy bar? You know I don't like you eating too much candy."

Hailey didn't answer me.

"Regardless, stealing is never acceptable. Heath, did you steal your sister's candy bar?"

Heath stuck out his lower lip in a show of belligerence. "No."

My phone rang, and I reached for it. Easton. Just what I needed right now. Hailey was yelling at Heath, and Heath turned his back on her and stomped to the only bedroom with her on his heels.

I had a splitting headache.

"You have to answer him, Caro. I'll take the kids to school."

With a resigned sigh, I pressed the answer button. "Hi."

"Wow. Don't sound so happy to hear from me. What time are we meeting and where?"

"Today isn't a good time. It'll have to wait."

"What? What do you mean?" Now one more person was pissed at me.

"I mean it's not a good time." I was reaching the end of my patience.

"What kind of game are you playing?"

I was playing a coward's game, getting cold feet, having second thoughts. I didn't want anyone else to have a say in my children's lives, but it was a little late for that. "No games. I promise."

"The condo should be ready in a day or so. As soon as I get the green light, I'll give you a tour, and some of the guys are going to help move you in this weekend."

"That's not necessary. I'll hire movers. I don't need your help."

"Not happening, Caro. I'll take care of the move. Quit jerking me around. You can't undo what's been done. I can't forget what I know. Neither can you."

"I understand, and I'm so sorry. Please, give me a little more time to adjust."

He was silent for so long I hoped he'd hung up. No such luck. He was still on the line. "Where shall I meet you? How about the hotel café?"

He wasn't going away. He was right; there was no turning back, only going forward.

"I'll see you at eleven," I said, resigned to my fate.

He ended the call without another word.

I sank down onto the couch, wondering what kind of monster I'd created.

Chapter Eleven

COMPLICATIONS

--Easton--

*L*ater that morning, I arrived early at the small café in the hotel my attorney had booked for Caro and our children. The hotel wasn't far from my condo, so I walked, enjoying a crisp fall day with clear skies.

I ordered a cup of coffee and stared out the window, more fidgety and nervous than I'd been in my first NHL game. This wasn't a game. This was life, and being a father was forever.

Caro stopped in the doorway and glanced around. I gulped down some water to ease my dry throat. She dropped something and bent down to pick it up. My eyes were drawn to her nicely rounded ass hugged by a pair of skinny jeans, and I swallowed hard. She still had an effect on me, and I had to get beyond what she did to me physically and see her merely as the mother of my children.

This situation was complicated enough without throwing a physical or emotional relationship with Caro into the mix. Her husband had only been dead a few months. She wasn't ready for a relationship, and I was a sworn bachelor, a Puck Brother. I didn't take my PB status lightly either. I'd earned it, and I would wear my badge proudly. I had to rein in my lust.

No complicated relationships, and a sexual relationship with her, even for one night, would be too complicated for my easygoing, do-as-I-please lifestyle. The woman planned her life and made lists while I wandered through life without a care or a worry.

Confusing shit, that was.

I wasn't one who dissected situations or worried about much of anything, but she had me so inside out I was doing both, and I didn't like the experience.

Seeing her again brought back old insecurities, and I could not allow a woman to jeopardize my pro career. I hadn't seven years ago, and I wouldn't now. I was absolutely committed to hockey, my team, and now my children. There wasn't room for anyone else in my life. Well, except my family, but they didn't demand much from me.

Steeling my shaky resolve, I plastered a neutral expression on my face and waited for Caro to walk in. I gripped the manila envelope stuffed with paperwork and waited for her to sit. Her gaze flicked from me to the envelope and back again. She had as good of a poker face as I.

"Easton." She spoke pleasantly, as if she were meeting a client for a business meeting, not a father to discuss their children. She placed a day planner on the table, and I recalled she'd always had one in her possession. No digital planners for her.

She looked fantastic and smelled as good as she looked. My gaze strayed downward, taking in those shapely legs encased in denim, and travelled upward. Her hips were wider and her breasts larger than I remembered. She had more curves than before even though she was still on the petite, slender side. Motherhood hadn't ruined her figure, it'd improved on it. I liked what I saw way too much.

I breathed in her unique scent and was flooded with memories of hot summer nights on the beach and in the back seat of my beat-up old Toyota. We'd gone at it those few months like the sex-crazed teenagers we were. There'd been quiet times, too. Lying on a blanket and gazing at the stars or talking about our hopes and dreams, mine all revolving around hockey, of course. Hers had been to use her full-ride scholarship to get a degree in nursing. I guess she'd never done it, which made me sad.

Caro cleared her throat, and I jerked my gaze away from her body. Embarrassed I'd been caught ogling her, I felt heat rise from my neck to my ears. If she'd noticed my flushed face, she gave no indication.

"I have the paperwork from my attorney for the temporary parenting plan." Flustered, I fumbled with the stapled sets of papers, giving her one copy, while I looked at the other. "I'll give you time to read it."

She said nothing but nodded. I ordered coffee, got a handle on myself, and sat back to observe her. She chewed on her lower lip as she read, a quirk she'd always had when concentrating on something important. I drew in a labored breath and was grateful the growing bulge between my legs wasn't visible because of the table. This was the mother of my children, not a woman I'd be getting naked with now or in the future.

Yet... I squelched those thoughts before they took root.

"Aren't you jumping the gun? They don't even know you're their father. They need time."

"I'm not asking for you to adhere to this immediately."

"I'm not sure about this visitation schedule," she said stiffly. Her gaze met mine, and she was in full mother-bear protective mode. "It's too many days."

"Too many days?" I fucking didn't think it was enough. My intention had been working my way slowly to joint custody, and she was questioning my initial request of a few days a week when I didn't have a road trip.

Houston, we have a fucking problem.

"I'm their mother. I know best." She glared stubbornly at me, her chin jutting out as she clenched it.

"I'm their father, and I have rights too," I shot back, equally stubborn and more than a little insulted. This woman was becoming a master at pushing my buttons.

"I don't want my children exposed to certain elements common in a pro hockey player's life."

"Elements? Like what?"

"A revolving door of women, for one, drugs and alcohol for another."

"That won't be an issue. I don't do drugs or have a revolving door of women." Hell, I hadn't wanted another woman since Caro came back. Now there was subject a shrink would love to explore, and I wasn't going there.

"You don't have roommates who're single hockey players? What about them?"

She had me there. "Uh, I do. Kaden and Steele. They're good guys. They'll behave when the kids are around."

"Have you discussed this with them?"

"Uh, not yet."

"Then how do you know they're willing to give up their decadent lifestyle when children are present?"

"Because they will, or I'll get my own place."

She sniffed and looked down her nose at me. I'd forgotten how much I hated it when she did that. She made a few notes in the back of her day planner. I leaned forward to read them, but she slammed the planner shut.

"I'm willing to do what it takes. I'll be by later this afternoon to meet the kids." I glowered at her. We were at a standoff, and we hadn't discussed any of the other points in the agreement. Unfortunately, my dick wasn't nearly as annoyed. In fact, my boy found her anger a turn-on and was begging for a chance. Damn it. This wasn't the time or place for lust, and my weakness for her annoyed the fuck out of me.

"It's too soon."

"In my opinion, it's way too late. See you around four thirty."

"We have plans. Come tomorrow."

"I have a game." I crossed my arms over my chest and gave her one of my intimidating hockey-player glares. She didn't even blink.

"Friday night then."

I wanted to argue. I didn't want to wait even one more hour, but two days? I didn't answer, but I stood, tossed a few bills on the table to cover the tab, and left before she had time to change her mind.

It was crucial we maintain an amicable relationship for the kids' sakes, not ours. While my parents had always presented a united front, I'd had too many friends whose parents used the kids to get back at the other parent. I would never do that. Never.

One way to maintain a cordial relationship with Caro was to stay out of her pants, yet every time I was around her, I wanted nothing but to strip off every stitch of clothing and plant myself deep inside her. She had always had some kind of sexual hold on me, and seven years later, she still did.

My self-control was infamous, but she tested not just my patience but my willpower to the limits.

--Caroline--

That afternoon the sunshine turned to rain, and the kids were getting cabin fever, edgy and distracted.

Some days they put aside their resentfulness and sorrow, behaving as they once had. Other days Heath barely spoke to me, and Hailey freely expressed her anger by directing it toward me. Today was one of those bad days. Despite my efforts to engage them, they chose to ignore me and played a video game. While I normally limited their playing time, on a crappy day like this, I was too tired to argue. Instead, I tortured myself by thinking of my earlier conversation with Easton.

Putting him off was stupid and irresponsible. My actions honestly made no sense, but I wasn't making a lot of sense lately. Two hours, two days, two weeks. What did it matter? Any timeframe would be too soon for my taste. Better to rip the Band-Aid off all at once and get it over with.

Still, I hedged. The sooner Easton got involved in the kids' lives, the more I'd see of him. I wasn't sure how I'd handle his presence in my kids' lives and, even worse, in mine.

Junie was doing her nails, while Rusty sprawled on the couch next to her. I slumped in the nearby chair. The thing was one of those uncomfortable hotel chairs that wouldn't be comfortable no matter how you sat in it.

"You need a glass of wine," Juniper said.

"Tell me about it. It's been a long day."

Junie sent a sympathetic smile in my direction and turned back to her nails, which she was painting a bright orange.

"Aren't you a little late for Halloween nails?"

"These are fall nails, you know, Thanksgiving colors."

I shrugged. "Whatever you say."

A sharp rap on the door startled both of us. Before we could react, Hailey leaped to her feet and scurried to the door. I yelled after her, but she ignored me. She knew better than to open the door to a stranger, but she was mad enough at me to ignore my warnings and do it anyway. I hurried after her, but she beat me to the door.

She swung the door wide open and stared at the large man taking up the majority of the doorway.

"Well, hi there." Easton grinned down at her.

Chapter Twelve

NOT ALONE

--Easton--

$\mathcal{T}$he little girl who gazed up at me was the spitting image of her beautiful mother. She had large blue eyes and long golden hair, while the stubborn set of her jaw reminded me of myself. She planted her little hands on her hips and narrowed those pretty eyes in what I interpreted as a hostile glare, so out of place on one so young.

Her obvious dislike at first sight set me back on my heels. In my naïve imaginings, I'd pictured her running up to me and launching her little body into my waiting arms. We'd laugh and hug, and I'd spin her around and around until we were both so dizzy, after which I'd have to collapse in the nearest chair. She'd call me Daddy, and my heart would fill up with love every time she said that one amazing word.

"Who are you?" she demanded. I blinked several times, unable to construct an explanation.

A little boy came to a stop behind her as if he had her back. He, too, planted little fists on his hips, legs slightly spread, and scowled at me. *My son.* Dark brown eyes, dark hair with a mind of its own, and a sturdy little body. He was mine, all right. I had no doubt they were both products of my genetics and Caro's. How had she not noticed sooner? Why hadn't she voiced her concerns to me as soon as their parentage became obvious? Why had she kept me in the dark? Caro was such a by-the-book person, I found it really hard to believe she hadn't a clue.

Anger simmered inside me. I'd tamped it down over the weeks, but now it was back full force. These were my children, and I had rights, too. Damn it, and damn her.

"Who are you?" my daughter, Hailey, demanded again and not very politely. She craned her neck way up to see me. I knelt down so I'd be at eye level.

"I'm Easton. I'm—" I glanced up at Caro, who hovered nearby. Her eyes pleaded with me, and I couldn't bring myself to be the asshole I'd planned to be. "I'm an old friend of your mother's."

Hailey's expression softened slightly, going from hostile to curious. "I'm Hailey, and this is my brother, Heath. We're twins but we don't look alike. Not like most twins. There were twins in my old school, and no one could tell them apart. They would pretend to be each other. Heath and I can't do that because I'm a girl and he's a boy, and we don't look anything alike. Were you friends with my father too? He's gone, you know. Mommy said he's gone to heaven, and he won't be back, but he's watching over us, and we have to make him proud. Do you have a mommy and daddy? Do you have a dog? We want a dog. I want a pony too. Do you like to ice skate? Heath and I ice skate. He plays hockey. I do figure skating. I'm the best figure skater in the world."

Holy shit. I struggled to keep up with her steady stream of words as she pounded me with a hundred questions and zero time to answer them. But damn, she was adorable, and I fell in love with her at first sight.

My baby girl.

My heart swelled, and I fought to control my emotions. How did a guy do that when he laid eyes on his children for the first time? I blinked back tears and slid my gaze to Caro. She stepped forward as soon as Hailey paused to draw a breath, put her hands on the little girl's shoulders, and squeezed.

"Hailey, slow down. Easton is very busy and regretfully doesn't have time to answer your questions."

"Actually, for you, sweetheart, I have all the time in the world." I winked at Hailey and grinned at Caro with evil pleasure, reveling in the disapproving scowl on her beautiful face.

"Well, we were just leaving, so if you don't mind, I need to get the kids' shoes on, or we'll be late." Caro attempted to move both children aside and away from me. Hell no, that wasn't happening, and the kids weren't budging, and neither was I.

I turned my attention to the boy, Heath.

"Hi, Heath, I'm Easton." I held out my hand. He stared at it for a moment, seeming to struggle with what to do next. He shook my hand and gawked at me. The kid had a firm handshake.

"We aren't going anywhere. You said so. You said we didn't have any money and had to stay home all weekend. Mr. E, would you stay and play with us?" Hailey challenged her mother while Heath continued to gawk at me, reminding me of the starstruck kids I'd met at team events. Did he realize who I was?

I smirked at Caro, having caught her in an out-and-out lie. She glared back at me.

"I'm sure Easton has better things to do with his time."

"Nope." I pushed past Caro and followed the kids into the living room. My disapproving gaze swept around the room and landed back on Caro.

"It's a little messy," she stammered.

"Junie? Hey, how are you?" I gave her a big hug. I'd met her that summer too. We'd hung out as a group and drunk beer and partied, typical teenage shit, which, if I were honest, I was still doing.

"Big E, you're looking hot as ever." She beamed at me, oblivious to the daggers being sent her way by her best friend.

The two kids stood nearby, watching the exchange in silence. Something rubbed up against my leg. I looked down and my grin grew wider.

"Rusty, my buddy!" I picked up the fat orange tabby and held him in my arms. He assaulted me with loud purrs and kneading claws in my arm. I remembered Caro's cat well. He and I often hung together, him on my lap demanding pets, and me complying. "How old is Rusty now?"

"Ten. Can we have a word?" Caro's words were clipped and tense. I grinned easily at her, knowing my mere presence was annoying her beyond belief, and my easygoing attitude made her even more irritated.

"Sure, what's up?" I placed Rusty on the nearest chair and shoved my hands in my pockets.

"Privately."

"Love to." I gave her the once-over, knowing she'd be ready to explode after my gaze raked up and down her body. She was madder than hell and stalked toward the open doorway. I leisurely followed her into the room and shut the door. I leaned against the door, my expression impassive.

She spun on me, her face contorted in rage. "What are you doing here?"

"Visiting my children, as I have a legal right to do," I answered calmly.

"I told you tonight wasn't a good night."

I merely cocked one eyebrow and crossed one ankle over the other.

"Easton, please, this is difficult."

"You're making it so."

"I'm worried about the twins. You don't have any idea what they've been through."

I frowned, pushing away a twinge of guilt. She was partially right, and I knew it as well as she.

"I'm sorry. I needed to see them. And I do know what they've been through. I lost my dad in a fire when I was ten. Remember?"

She deflated before my very eyes, as if all her courageous blustering had been nothing but hot air and someone had poked a hole in it. She looked down, but not before I caught her lower lip quivering.

Oh, crap, she was going to cry. I couldn't handle tears. We were doing quite well sniping at each other; why'd she have to ruin it by crying and revealing her vulnerability?

"Please, just leave." She lifted her head, and that beautiful face contorted in agony, and I'd done this to her. I should've been an asshole and merely shrugged, but I wasn't made like that. I was basically a good guy, and she was getting to me in ways only she could. A tear slid down one high cheekbone and dropped off her chin, followed by another and another.

Fuck. I wasn't strong enough to walk away—at least not when it came to her.

In two steps, I pulled her into my arms, engulfing her with my much larger body. At first, she was stiff as a hockey stick. I stroked her back and just let her be, and she relaxed into me. Her arms went around my neck, as if it were the most natural thing in the world, and once it had been. Great shuddering sobs racked her thin body, and she clung to me as if I were her lifeline. The Caro I'd known had been so strong, so independent. Seeing her broken like this wrecked me.

"Caro, I'm truly sorry. We can work this out. I'll do it your way for now if only you'll let me spend a little time with them. I want to get to know my kids."

She blubbered into my shirt, and the wetness from her tears soaked through to my skin. I was sick with concern and worry. Right now, all I wanted to do was protect her, but from who? From me?

Finally, she gazed up at me, her eyes red and swollen, tracks of tears on her face. "I'm sorry. I'm so scared. So very scared. I feel all alone."

"You're not alone anymore. I'm here now."

What the hell had I just committed to?

Chapter Thirteen

SHOW ME

--Caroline--

hy did I show weakness to a man who held all the cards while I held nothing but a joker?

I'd fallen into his arms too easily. Being surrounded by his big, strong body felt too right, too good, too dangerous. He was bigger than he had been as a teenager. His body was harder and more muscular. He'd matured into a very attractive man, and the woman in me was all in. Thank God my head was still in charge of my body, or so I hoped.

I had the kids to consider. They were my priority. Starting any kind of relationship with this man endangered that priority and muddied the waters, not to mention what it did for my sanity and their well-being.

I placed my hands on his chest and pushed him away. He backed off without protest but kept his fingers wrapped loosely around my arms.

He opened his mouth to say something, but Hailey burst into the room, followed, as usual, by her wingman, Heath.

"Mr. E, are you going to play a video game with us?" She stared up at him with big, wide eyes. My little girl was already drawn to this man, her father, and my throat clogged with an unexplainable emotion. I didn't have a clue what it was I felt, but it was pleasant and unpleasant at the same time.

Easton glanced at me for permission.

"If you have time," I said.

"I have time." His grin was wide, reminding me of Heath's last Christmas morning.

"Oh, good!" Hailey clapped her hands together and grabbed his big hand. She shot a glare at me, as if to say, *Don't you mess this up*. She knew something was off about Easton being just a friend. Call it child's intuition, but my perceptive little girl was suspicious.

The two of them walked out the bedroom door together, Easton's big hand engulfing her small one. Heath stared at me momentarily, and I feared he saw too much with those old eyes of his. Without a word, he trailed out the door after them.

My stomach clenched into a tight knot. Only then did I recognize the emotion sliding through me like a snake through the grass.

I was afraid of losing my kids to their father.

--Easton--

I didn't stay long, ever mindful of taking my relationship with my kids one step at a time and navigating the minefield of dealing with Caro. She'd turned cold again when I'd gone back to the living room. Fuck if I knew what I'd done this time to piss her off.

I might as well not agonize over her feelings since I couldn't please her anyway. This was about me and my kids. Not her. Worrying about her feelings would only get in the way of what I wanted for the twins and me, as it was obvious Caro didn't want it.

I played one game with chatty Hailey while Heath stayed in the background, never saying a word and always watching. I learned Hailey loved the color pink—no surprise there—wanted a pony in the worst way, was able to read to herself, hated Brussels sprouts—that we had in common—and loved to ice-skate. She was working on her spins. She was all girl, but she had my competitive spirit.

My attempts to draw Heath into the conversation failed miserably. He would shrug and say nothing. A glance at their hovering mother indicated she didn't have any better luck than me. In fact, I recalled she'd mentioned he'd been noncommunicative since his father died, except for when he was playing hockey.

Yeah, they were my kids. Genetics played a much larger role in our personalities than humans cared to admit. The twins hadn't been raised around me, yet each of them had aspects of my personality, for example, their love of all things skating.

I let myself into my condo. Kaden was sprawled on one side of the sectional couch, eating as usual and watching the Food Channel. He had his phone in one hand as he popped buffalo wings into his mouth with the other. Steele was on his laptop, oblivious to the rest of the world.

They both looked up as I walked in and threw myself down on the middle piece of the huge sectional. I was grinning from ear to ear. I couldn't help myself. I'd spent time, however brief, with my kids—my flesh and blood.

"Must've gone well?" Kaden licked his fingers and wiped them on a paper towel. He held the bowl of wings out to me, and I gladly snagged a few.

"Fucking incredible. I'm a dad. Guys, I'm a dad." With a chicken wing in each hand, I used them to punctuate every syllable.

"I find that scary as shit, but I'm happy for you. If one of my ladies told me I had a baby, I'd be freaking out," Kaden said.

"I am a little," I admitted. "It's a heavy responsibility."

"That's awesome, man," Steele, a man of very few words, said. He grabbed a wing from the bowl and chewed on it, deep in thought but not adding anything else to his comment. He'd been more secretive than usual lately, and I knew better than to pry. Steele was the most private person I'd ever known. He didn't even talk about his conquests unless he was wasted.

Meanwhile, the Puck Bros knew all the sordid details about Kaden's various hookups, even when we'd prefer not to know.

"Does Caro know you're moving her into a condo across the hall from us?"

"Not yet," I admitted.

Steele arched his brows but didn't reply. He shrugged and focused his attention back on his laptop. Kaden and I had speculated multiple times about what he found so fascinating that his head was always buried in that laptop. Not even a phone or tablet, but a laptop. Kaden, being a horndog, was certain it was kinky porn. I didn't think so, but who the hell knows. People could have some surprising secrets. I suspected whatever he was doing was more personal and private than porn. I liked to think he was writing the next great American novel or something profound. That's what I'd expect from such a quiet, intro-spective guy.

"She'll kick your ass," Kaden said.

"Yeah, I know, but I want them close." I stole the remote from Kaden and flipped through the channels for a hockey game, ignoring his protests. He had a TV in his room. He could watch that. There'd be a disadvantage to having them so close, such as having Caro across the hall and attempting to resist her. The other would be exposing my kids to the Puck Brothers. The thought sent chills up and down my spine. Not a good idea, but they weren't bad guys. I'd threaten them with bodily harm if they did anything unacceptable in front of my kids. Kaden would have to restrict his fucking of random women to his bedroom, instead of wherever he felt like it whenever he felt like it.

"Why aren't you out tonight?" I asked, suddenly curious.

"He met someone," Steele said. I glanced his direction, but he'd gone back to his laptop. Steele knew everything. The guy had heard it all and mostly kept the gossip to himself. I swung my attention back to Kaden, who was scowling at Steele. That was odd. Kaden loved talking about his sexual conquests.

"You met someone and because of that you're staying home?"

"It's a long story. She's busy tonight. Some kind of family obliga-tion." Kaden sounded grumpy.

"And you couldn't find anyone else willing to scratch your itch?"

"Something like that."

"What kind of Puck Brother, are you?" I teased.

"I could ask you the same thing? When's the last time you've hooked up with a random?"

"Not that long ago. More recent than you," I shot back. I'd enjoyed my brief stint in the league before Caro had initiated contact with me.

"He's addicted to this woman, like a drug. A bad drug." Steele met my gaze and rolled his eyes.

"You are?" I turned to Kaden, shocked this was the first I'd been hearing about it.

"She's hot, really hot, and adventurous in bed, and I can't fucking get enough of her."

"You falling for her? 'Cause that would mean you'd be the first to lose the bet," I said.

"No, I'm not," Kaden said defensively. "It's just sex. It's not like I found the woman I want to spend the rest of my life with, if I ever do."

"I see. Thanks for the clarification."

"I'm obsessed with her. I've tried to hook up with a few others, but none of them do what she does to me. I mean, she's game for anything. Absolutely anything. The fucking part that sucks is that she's really coy about when we can hook up, keeps me dangling. Doesn't want to be seen with me. Just wants to hook up."

"Maybe she's married," Steele suggested.

"She's not married. I asked her. She might have a boyfriend, not sure."

"Sounds like you're playing with fire, buddy. People keep secrets for a reason." I clapped him on the shoulder as I walked by, heading to the kitchen for a beer.

I'd never seen Kaden so wrapped up in a woman. He was the love-'em-and-leave-'em type. He didn't get attached. This wasn't an attachment though, sounded more like a sexual obsession. I didn't worry too much about it. Knowing Kaden, no matter how hot this woman was, the relationship would soon run its course.

Chapter Fourteen

MR. E

--Caroline--

On Saturday morning, I dragged my tired butt out of bed and cooked breakfast. I'd expected to hear from Easton by now. He'd texted yesterday that the condo was supposed to be ready to move into this weekend, but they were having issues getting a few repairs done.

"When is Mr. E coming to see us again?" Hailey asked. She held her ragged teddy bear in one hand and a worn book in the other. The teddy bear had been a gift from Mark, and my heart squeezed every time I saw it.

It'd been a few days since Easton had interrupted our afternoon and disrupted our lives. Hailey chattered nonstop about Mr. E, while Heath said nothing.

They didn't seem to know Easton was a hockey player, even though Heath did follow some pro hockey. If he did know, he wasn't talking, and I wasn't ready to tell them yet.

"When is he coming again?" Hailey insisted, not to be deterred.

"Soon. He's a very busy man. Please don't get your hopes up."

She sucked her lower lip into her mouth and blinked back tears. The tears came easily to her these past few months, and seeing them so often broke my heart. She'd been such a happy, carefree, loving child before Mark died.

"He said he'd watch me skate."

"He did?" I didn't conceal my surprise. I hadn't heard him say any such thing. He must have made the offer when I'd left briefly to use the bathroom.

Hailey nodded vigorously. "Didn't he, Heath?"

Heath's gaze flicked from me to Hailey and back to me. He nodded solemnly.

"I'm sure he will then." I suppressed a resigned sigh. My daughter was attaching herself to Easton already as a surrogate father, and the irony in the situation wasn't lost on me. Still, I worried Easton might not be around long term. He'd play the father role until he tired of it or some gorgeous celebrity caught his eye and he forgot he had kids.

I'd researched him pretty extensively the past few weeks, trying to get a handle on what kind of man he was now compared to the teenager I'd known. What I'd discovered were countless pictures of him with beautiful women on his arm, getting wasted with his buddies, and playing hockey. Of course, hockey. With Easton, hockey came first. And if he was traded to another team, then what would happen? I didn't see such a thing happening this season or even in the next couple years, but hockey players moved from team to team, and eventually Easton would, too. I wasn't following him all over North America with my kids in tow.

Kids survived moving around a lot. Other hockey families dealt with these issues, not to mention military families. I might as well admit it. I was the one who didn't want uprooted. Not that I had to. We weren't a couple or anything. But the one stipulation in the agreement stated we had to live within forty-five minutes of each other. What if I had a boyfriend or a husband? This requirement was unreasonable, and the paperwork wouldn't be signed until we straightened this out.

Resisting Easton's involvement in my children's lives was becoming futile, almost as futile as resisting his intrusion into my life.

"Hey, it's not raining. I'm going for a walk. Who wants to join me?" Junie announced as she entered the living room carrying the twins' coats, already knowing their answer. Hailey shot to her feet, jumping up and down and jabbering away. Heath stood, too, and reached for his coat.

"Caro? You coming?"

"If you don't mind, I have some things to finish up. I think I'll stay here."

Junie smiled and herded her charges out the door. She glanced over her shoulder just before she shut the door. "Enjoy your moments of silence."

"I will."

--Easton--

On Saturday morning, I worked out and attended the optional skate. By noon I was knocking, unannounced, on Caro's door. I was sure I'd piss her off again for not texting, but I was on a mission.

I had a game tonight, so my time was limited. Just this morning, the building manager had dropped off the keys to Caro's condo. The place was finally move-in ready. I'd taken the liberty of rounding up some teammates with trucks to move her in tomorrow.

The door flew open, and my baby girl stood on the other side. My grin was wider than the Columbia upon seeing my daughter. Her hair was a wild mess of curls, and there was a smudge of what looked like strawberry jam on her left cheek. She was so fucking adorable. I fell even more in love with her.

"Mr. E!" Hailey shrieked and held her arms out to me. I picked her up and spun her around without thinking. I caught Caro's scowl in my peripheral vision. Realizing my behavior might be over the top for a man who barely knew the twins, I set her down quickly. Hailey didn't seem to notice or care. Heath, as usual, stood silently watching, almost expectant. I hesitated, briefly considering whether or not I should pick him up and spin him around. He was so much more reserved than his sister, I decided against any huge displays of affection at this point in time.

"Hey, buddy." I winked at him and was rewarded with a lopsided grin. I was making progress.

"Mr. E! Mr. E!" Hailey tugged on my arm to get my attention.

"Call me Easton, honey."

I turned to Caro. Her annoyance was palpable, like a living, breathing thing permeating the room with her displeasure. She glared at me over the kids' heads.

"Easton, what a surprise."

I heard her message loud and clear. I hadn't called first—again. Well, fuck that. I wasn't playing games with her. Been there, tired of that. I'd damn well drop in and see my kids if I chose to, even as I admitted my behavior might be a little childish and disrespectful of her privacy. I wasn't winning any points with her, and perhaps that was my goal. If she hated me, she'd keep her distance.

I strolled into the living room as if I owned it, one hand on each of the twins' backs as I guided them to the middle of the room. I shot Caro a cocky grin as I passed. The woman was going to kill me or have insanely wild sex with me. I wasn't sure which one, though I'd put my money on death by slow torture.

"Hey, Junie, how ya doing?"

"I'm doing great." Junie grinned at me and rose from the battered couch to hug me.

Caro fumed next to us, but we both ignored her and carried on like the old friends we were—somewhat.

"I have some great news for you guys," I said, addressing my children.

"Oh, what is it?" Hailey jumped up and down. "Do you get me a pony, Mr. E. Did you? Did you? I've been a good girl, and I deserve a pony. I really do. A gray one with dapples and a long mane and tail. One that can run and jump and take me places. Please, oh, please, say you got me a pony? I love ponies. I love, love, love ponies."

I smiled down at her. "Not that kind of news. Besides, Christmas is coming. You'll have to wait to see what your present is." I avoided Caro's gaze, knowing she was seething inside and assuming I was leading her daughter on. I wasn't. In fact, a small seed grew as I considered how I'd go about getting my daughter a pony.

"So, what is it?" Junie asked, stopping Hailey before she erupted into another lava flow of words.

I held up a set of house keys and jangled them in front of their eyes. "You guys wanna see your new home?"

"We have a new place to live? Can Rusty go with us? Do we have to change schools? Do we—"

I was ready for Hailey this time and held a finger to my lips. "Slow down, sweetheart. One question at a time. My brain doesn't work as fast as yours, so we have to limit it to one question at a time. Let me see if I can remember them all."

Hailey stood on tiptoes and watched me with sparkling eyes. I rubbed my chin, as if deep in thought.

"You want to bring your pet turtle with you?"

Hailey giggled. "No, silly. Our cat, Rusty."

"You can do that." I grinned, and she lit up like the Christmas tree in Rockefeller Center. "And you won't have to change schools. It's only a few miles from here."

"Is it near my hockey rink?" Heath asked, surprising all of us with his question.

"It's not far. It's big and has a lot of room to play. There's a park nearby."

"When can we see it? When? When?" Hailey was jumping up and down with the kind of excitement only Hailey could show.

"Right now. I have the SUV parked outside. We'll all fit in it."

"Easton, can I have a word with you?"

Oh, God, not again. Caro's tone was short and clipped. Oh, yeah, I was in deep shit and wading deeper with every step.

"Sure, then we can see the apartment."

Caro stalked down the hall, and I followed in what was beginning to be a familiar routine for us and not a pleasant one either.

She turned on me like a wounded beast the second the door clicked shut. "What part of calling first do you not understand?"

"Obviously, all of it." I smirked at my clever response, despite knowing it'd send her into orbit.

She leaned into me, her sexy body vibrating with barely controlled fury. I seemed to bring the worst out in her, but her anger was hot as hell. Imagine all that extreme emotion directed into something more positive.

"You're being very ungrateful."

"You can't dictate my life."

"I'm not. I'm dictating my children's lives. You happen to be in the way."

Her nostrils flared with her temper. Stupid choice of words on my part, but I loved poking the lioness.

I moved closer to her, and she skittered backward a few steps, some of her anger turning to nervousness. "You're fucking sexy when you're mad at me. Remember when you thought I was flirting with that other girl, and you were so furious with me? Best fucking sex ever."

Her face softened a little, and I guessed she was remembering, too. We'd done it that night hot, hard, rough, totally down and dirty. When I said it'd been the best sex ever, I wasn't kidding. But then every time I'd fucked Caro, I'd thought it was the best sex ever.

"Fucking sex, isn't that redundant?" A ghost of a smile played on her lips. My gaze slid down her face to those lips. I wanted to taste their sweetness once again. This invisible thread of attraction had always connected us, and it tugged me closer. I leaned into her, and she leaned into me. I brushed my lips against hers and heard her throaty gasp. God, that was sexy as fuck. My fingers wrapped around the back of her neck, and I pulled her close for a deeper kiss. She didn't resist but kissed me right back, opening up to me. Our tongues mated, our lips talked to each other without talking but using the oldest language known to man. I closed my eyes, giving myself up to the emotions being set free inside me. I felt her as if she were a part of me, while the world spun lazily around us and wrapped us in its protective arms. For one short moment, my life was complete, perfect, just as it should be.

These weren't the crazed kisses of teenagers with raging hormones, but they were the crazed kisses of two adults with epic sexual chemistry. In the years Caro and I had been apart, through all the girlfriends and hookups, nothing felt like this. Absolutely fucking nothing.

We'd always been like this together, and time hadn't dampened our desire for each other.

Breathing as hard as if I'd sprinted around the ice arena twenty times, I drew back and nuzzled her neck and collarbone. She smelled like honey and flowers and better days with even better nights. She smelled like she was mine, and I was hers.

Only she wasn't. She'd been someone else's for years. She wasn't my Caro anymore.

The moment ended too quickly, but I still wanted her any way I could get her. Even the reality of her situation didn't drown out the raw need she'd set loose inside me.

"Easton," she sighed against my ear, "we can't do this. We can't—"

We both froze at the knock on the door.

"Not again," I grumbled and backed away with reluctance.

"Come in," Caro said in a shaky voice.

"Hey, am I interrupting?" Juniper said through the closed door.

"Yes, you are," I said, ignoring Caro's murderous glare. "We're in the middle of something."

"We are not. Please, come in."

Juniper entered. Her knowing smirk said it all as she shifted her gaze from one of us to the other. "I was interrupting something. I knew it."

We weren't fooling her, and I didn't expect to. The chemistry between us was too strong, too transparent, and impossible to mask. Neither Caro nor I was good at subterfuge. Hopefully, the kids didn't notice.

Red faced, Caro looked away, while I grinned.

"I'm really excited about seeing our new apartment, E, and I wanted to make sure Caro wasn't being ungracious, as she tends to be, and telling you to shove those keys up your ass."

"She is, but I'm ignoring her."

"Where is this condo exactly?" Caro asked through gritted teeth.

"Not far from here. In my building."

"In your building?" She gave me one of those *are you crazy* glances and groaned. Yeah, I was crazy. Crazy stupid or crazy smart. Only time would tell.

"Yup. It's safe and clean and big, and on the same floor as mine."

"The same floor?"

"Directly across the hall." I grinned guilelessly as if I expected her to be thrilled when I knew she really wanted to feed me to the lions at Woodland Park Zoo.

"Wonderful, just wonderful."

"I thought it was." I grinned, and Junie and I fist-bumped.

My gaze drifted to Caro. She was still flushed, and her lips were parted slightly, reminding me how good it felt to have those lips on mine. I wanted them again and again and again. Avoiding a sexual relationship with her was going to be the hardest thing I ever did, and I wasn't sure I was up to the task.

Chapter Fifteen

DELUSIONAL

--Caroline--

Reluctantly, and having zero say in the matter, I loaded the kids and myself into Easton's big-assed luxury SUV. That thing could haul Heath's entire hockey team and all their gear. I sat in the back seat with the kids while Juniper sat in the front seat with Easton. She jabbered as much as Hailey did, going on and on about the condo and how excited she was and couldn't wait to see it.

Easton pulled into a parking garage on the bottom level of a tall building with walls of windows. We took the elevator up several levels. To be honest, I didn't notice what level he punched. I was too busy staring at his profile as he lovingly gazed down at my...our children. His protective yet affectionate expression almost brought me to my knees in that confined space. I propped myself up against the wall, faking a casual stance. Easton never once glanced my way, his attention focused on our kids. If I'd stripped naked and dry-humped him, I'm not sure he would've noticed. A strangled giggle erupted from my throat, and Junie gave me a questioning look.

"Nothing," I said. She shrugged and didn't press for details.

The elevator door swished open. Much to my surprise, Easton glanced over his shoulder as he ushered the kids into the hallway. He cocked a brow at me, and without thinking, I threw him a saucy kiss. His brown eyes darkened for a moment, and I knew what he was thinking because I was thinking—and wanting—the same thing.

Hailey tugged on his arm, diverting his attention. He swung her up onto his broad shoulders with ease. She screeched with joy and giggled. They headed down the hall with Junie beside them, both females keeping up a steady stream of conversation while Easton grinned from ear to ear.

Heath stared at them wistfully. I reached for his hand, and our eyes met momentarily. I was struck by the longing in his dark eyes and slammed by the realization he was feeling left out and a little jealous.

Welcome to the club, my young man.

I squeezed his hand and together we trailed after the boisterous group.

At the end of a long, wide hall, Easton stopped before a large door. He turned a key in the lock and nudged the door open with his foot. He lifted Hailey off his shoulders, and she ran ahead of us into the condo. Heath wriggled his hand free and ran after her.

Easton didn't venture a glance my way, almost as if he'd forgotten about me. Junie and he entered the condo, leaving me alone in the hallway. Prodding myself into action, I hurried after them and closed the door behind me before turning to survey my surroundings.

I hadn't expected furnishings. I had a storage unit full of stuff.

But this place...

The windows went from floor to ceiling with expansive views. This side of the building didn't have a water view, but the views were spectacular regardless.

The kitchen was all black granite and white cabinetry with large stainless-steel appliances. The open floor plan boasted a spacious living room and dining area, much larger than I'd have expected in a condo. The floors were a gleaming hardwood of some kind, and I was certain they were real wood. Laminate wouldn't grace a place like this.

Junie and the kids headed down the hallway toward the bedrooms and bathrooms. I grabbed Easton's arm. He turned, regarding me curiously.

"This is too much. We can't afford this."

"You don't have to." He tried to extract his arm from my grip, but I held on tightly.

"Easton. I can't allow you to pay for a luxury condo with a view."

"I didn't ask you to allow me. I'm doing it. These are my children." He set his jaw stubbornly, a sure sign there'd be zero arguing with him. His expression softened slightly. "Listen, don't worry. The team owner owns this building. This condo is ours for the next six months until a relative of his retires and moves back to Seattle. That'll give us enough time to find something suitable."

"But the furniture... The kids will destroy it."

Easton glanced around as if he'd just noticed the place was furnished with gray and white furniture, sure to show sticky finger-prints. He shrugged. "We'll cross that bridge when it's time. If I have to replace a few pieces, I will."

"I don't think this is a good idea."

"I do. I'm trying to make up for six lost years. The kids will be close by. I'll get to see them a lot."

"And your place is across the hall?"

"*Directly* across the hall." He grinned wickedly at me, and I read his mind—close enough for a late-night visit to my room while everyone else was sleeping—or perhaps my own sexually deprived brain imag-ined I was reading his mind. Most likely I was reading my own mind.

All those years ago, I'd been living at home, and Easton had been living with a billet family for the summer. We didn't have the luxury of a private space to have sex. We'd been quite adventurous back then. I missed those pre-adulting days of minor responsibility and major fun, not that I'd trade my memories with my kids for anything, but sometimes...

I let that thought drift away. Easton stared at me expectantly. He must've asked me a question, but for the life of me, I didn't have a clue what it might be.

"I'm sorry, what?"

"Do you want to see the bedrooms? Most of the condos only have two or three bedrooms. This one has four, a big plus if you ask me. You'll each have your own room."

The luxury of my own space wasn't lost on me.

He grabbed my hand and led me down the hallway, as excited as a kid on Christmas morning. He moved to the first open doorway. "This bedroom and the one at the end of the hall have en-suite bathrooms. The two bedrooms in the middle share a bathroom, which would be perfect for the kids."

"My own bathroom?" I'd been sharing one bathroom with Junie and the kids for a little too long.

"Yeah, with a big soaking tub." He winked at me and ran his gaze hungrily down my body and back up again. I shivered and hugged myself, following him into the spacious though not overly large room. The bathroom was all black granite and white tile with a walk-in tiled shower and a large jetted bathtub. I'd spend hours in there with a good book or, even better, a good man.

My gaze slid to Easton, who had his back to me. He turned and caught me gawking at him. I turned away quickly, but he had to see the longing in my eyes.

--Easton--

Moving Caro and Co. to the condo across the hall was a stroke of genius. I'd have all the time I needed to assess the situation and figure out a game plan.

I'd seen a few things that disturbed me and raised red flags. My son was shut down and closed off, for one, and my daughter directed a large amount of anger toward her mother. I remembered how much I'd blamed my mom after my dad had died. If only my mom had insisted my dad not pick up that extra shift instead of telling him the family could use the money since Christmas was coming. My misplaced anger had been unfair to her, but anger was one of the stages of grief.

Hailey was running up and down the hall with Heath hurrying after her. He was actually smiling. They'd both claimed their rooms and were planning all sorts of kid stuff.

I handed Caro one set of keys and Junie the other.

"I have a game tonight, but I got a few guys together to move you in tomorrow."

"I'll need to assess what can be moved from storage and what can't."

"I'm sure you'll do that. Does noon give you enough time?"

"Beggars can't be choosers. I'll make it work."

Junie threw her arms around me and hugged me tightly. "Thank you, thank you, thank you. If you ever need anything, I'm a fantastic baker. Let me know."

"You can bake for me anytime."

Caro stepped forward. I saw the battle in her eyes. She didn't like how I'd handled this situation, not asking her first, but she sighed resignedly. I held out my arms for a hug, and she shook her head.

"Thank you, Easton. You've been very kind." Her words were stiff and formal. I fought hard not to laugh. A few hours ago, we'd been on the verge of going at it on her bed while the kids and Junie were one wall away. At least in this condo, there'd be more room, and I knew from experience—thank you, Kaden—the rooms were well sound-proofed.

"You're welcome. It's my pleasure."

I met her gaze and held it. Despite all my protests to the contrary, I couldn't come up with one good reason not to have a sexual relation-ship with the mother of my children, at least not one I wouldn't throw out the window given half a chance. We were hot for each other. We weren't seeing anyone else. There was nothing to stop us. We were both old enough to know the difference between sex and love, even if we hadn't as teenagers.

If both of us understood the mutual benefits of hooking up without emotional strings, what would be the harm?

Yeah, what would be the harm?

I'd been a kid and thought I'd loved her once. I'd broken into a million pieces when I'd walked away from her, yet I'd done it not just for my career but hers. She'd wanted to go to nursing school. Following a hockey player around from team to team didn't make such an education feasible.

I'd done the right thing by leaving her. Should I do the right thing by leaving her alone?

Maybe, but I couldn't.

Ever since she'd come back into my life, that emptiness had faded. I felt purpose, I felt happy, and I felt something I hadn't felt in years. Yeah, I was a new father, but those kids weren't the entire reason my life had turned around.

Right now I had everything I'd ever wanted, and I was fucking hanging on to it with all the determination and grit I possessed.

I wasn't talking about a long-term relationship or even love, just a great sexual relationship without all the emotional encumbrances, drama, and heartache I associated with a full-blown relationship.

A few days ago, I'd sworn to keep my hands off Caro. Today, I was plotting how to get those hands all over her hot little body.

If I didn't know better, I'd say I was a hot mess like Kaden, but I wasn't. I was in control, not being controlled by a woman.

Or I was fucking delusional.

Chapter Sixteen

SHAMELESS

--Caroline--

I had to admit the truth.

I looked forward living in the spiffy new condo for the next several months. And if I was really honest with myself, being across the hall from Easton wasn't so bad either—primarily so the kids would have easy access to their father, of course. Nothing to do with me.

Junie and I packed up the hotel room first, which didn't take too long. Then we headed to the storage unit and began the arduous task of separating out what stayed in storage and what moved to the condo. The kids sat in the car, read on their tablets, and took naps. I had everything ready by the time the first truck pulled up next to the unit.

As truck after truck arrived, I stood in awe at the sheer manpower filing into the small space. Boxes were lifted and hauled out with incredible efficiency. These guys were used to working together on the ice, and that teamwork spread to packing out boxes, too.

I did my share. I never believed in being one of those women who stood by and watched the men do the heavy lifting. I held my own. Easton attempted to relieve my load multiple times, but I'd hear nothing of it.

Within a few hours, everything that needed to be moved was loaded.

Having a professional hockey player as the father of my children did have its advantages.

The procession of trucks pulled up outside Easton's building, and we did the entire thing all over again. This time I didn't carry in boxes but directed where each item should go as per the careful notes I'd placed on each box.

Easton had pizza delivered, and his roommate Kaden lugged in a few cases of beer. The living room burst at the seams with lounging hockey players, the aroma of pizza, and boisterous laughter. Junie and I had been introduced to the half-dozen guys who'd shown up, but I didn't recall all the names. Many of them lived in this building since it was close to the practice facility and the team owner gave them a good deal on long-term leases. Ethan Parker had bought the property and built the condos with the intention of housing his hockey players here, especially the single ones. Most of the married players opted for large homes with yards.

Junie flirted shamelessly with the guys while I observed her amusing performance. She had these guys eating out of her hand, and I suspected she'd been propositioned by more than a few of them.

Steele and the kids were playing a board game at the dining room table. Every once in a while, Steele would groan, and the kids would giggle. They were handing Steele his ass on a platter, or so it sounded.

Easton stuck close to me while participating in the banter going back and forth. He'd told them about the twins, and no one thought it was odd he was paying so much attention to me. No one but me, that is.

For a brief moment, I allowed myself to be transported back to a time when we were teenagers and had our entire future ahead of us. It'd been a time of hope and happiness. Being with Easton opened up an entirely different life than I'd had in the past. He was from a good family with two great brothers and a loving mother. I'd met them a few times when they'd come to watch him play. His mother was a gem, and Easton talked fondly of his father.

I'd been drawn to Easton because he was self-confident, easygoing, and rarely flustered. He enjoyed life and didn't worry much about his future. I was the opposite. I'd vowed to make something of myself. I'd show my parents. They told me I'd never be anything but a failure and would end up barefoot and pregnant by the time I was eighteen. How prophetic.

I had ended up pregnant and neither parent had been the least bit supportive. My father told me to get an abortion, and my mother booted me out of the house. She didn't want any screaming brats underfoot. I was on my own, except for Mark. He stepped up and married me, rescuing me from a fate I'd sworn never to succumb to.

Mark loved the kids, probably more than me. He didn't bat an eye when we found out I was having twins. The prospect excited him. His parents were hugely supportive, unlike mine, who to this day had never shown any interest in meeting their grandchildren.

Those early days had been wonderful. I'd loved Mark, not with the white-hot passion I'd had with Easton, but with an easy, secure love. We'd been happy together. I adored his parents. They'd been supportive and loving toward the twins. I saw them as role models of good parenting.

The last couple years hadn't been bad, but looking back, I'd been complacent and in a rut. I gave up my dreams and busted my ass trying to be the good little wife and measuring up to my own high expectations. I was a girl from the wrong side of the tracks. That alone was a huge strike against me in my opinion, not that Mark or his parents cared one damn bit, but I did. Being that girl had always defined me and driven me to be the best, whether it was student, mother, or wife.

"Hey, penny for your thoughts?"

I blinked a few times, focusing on Easton. He held out a copper penny. I shrugged. No way in hell was I discussing my innermost secrets with him.

"You were so deep in thought, you didn't hear a thing I said."

"I'm sorry. What did you say?"

"Let's see how things go for the next few months, then we'll decide on a permanent agreement."

"I like that idea." The skeptic in me wondered what his angle was. Throughout my life, the people who were supposed to love me used me for their own selfish gain. I hadn't gone to college because Mark had asked me to wait until the kids were in school. I hadn't paid attention to finances because Mark insisted on taking care of everything. I hadn't done anything for me because of an underlying belief I wasn't good enough.

I refused to play the victim though. I'd learned my lessons. This time no one would manipulate me or guilt me into doing things that didn't benefit my life or my children's lives, even if that person was Easton.

"Good," he said with his easygoing grin. "I know you'll be more comfortable with something in writing. I'm fine with winging it, but that's not how you like to do things."

After all these years, Easton still knew me too well. I'd been a dot-the-i's-and-cross-the-t's kind of person, controlling any aspect of my life I'd been able to control by being super-organized. I was still like that. Hell, I'd color-coded and labelled every box and item so my moving crew would know exactly where it went. If that wasn't over-organized, I didn't know what was.

Easton stepped closer to me until I felt the heat from his body. I didn't move. My feet were anchored to the floor. We didn't touch, but my body reacted as if we had. Every nerve ending was supercharged and hyperaware of the sexy man standing merely inches away. If there hadn't been people nearby, I'd have jumped him, ripped off his clothes, and fucked his gorgeous brains out, despite my vows not to do so. My gaze dropped to his jeans and the telltale bulge pressing against his fly. He wanted me, too. No doubt about that. Slowly, I ran my gaze up his body, not caring that I was caught admiring him. He'd had an amazing physique as a teenager. I couldn't imagine what he'd look like naked now. Okay, I lied. I did imagine what he looked like every single night when I lay in bed. I did pleasure myself to thoughts of him, rather than Mark. The disloyalty of such acts wasn't lost on me, but Mark wasn't here, and he was never coming back.

"Caro?" Easton's deep voice pulled my attention away from his broad chest and my guilty thoughts. "You okay?"

"I'm fine," I said tightly.

"We'll make this work, Caro." Easton lowered his voice so only I could hear, not that anyone was paying attention to us.

Make what work? Was he referring to co-parenting or something more?

--Easton--

Thanksgiving came and went. I had a fantasy Caro and me and the kids would have our first Thanksgiving together. We did not. I went to Coop and Izzy's instead, while Caro insisted on a private Thanksgiving as it was the twins' first major holiday without Mark.

I wasn't happy about her decision, but I wasn't in a position to do much about it either. In some ways, I had to admit she was right, but from a personal point of view, I guess I was butt-hurt at being excluded from their holiday. Christmas would not happen like this.

The Sockeyes played home games both the day before and day after Thanksgiving. I was pretty busy, and despite their proximity to my doorway—about fifteen feet—I didn't see much of Caro and Co. until the following week. They also needed time to pack and settle in. Even though I was itching to start what I considered my new life as a father, I backed off, giving them the necessary space.

The following Monday, Caro and I sat at the shiny black dining room table in her new condo and hashed out the details of a temporary agreement. Tomorrow I left on a four-day road trip.

Caro made notes in the margins of the paperwork, and I craned my neck to read what she'd written. She caught me in the act, and I looked away, ashamed of myself for reading her personal notes.

The sooner we had this agreement done, the better. I'd legally have rights to see my kids. Caro had agreed to allow me to see the twins whenever I was available as long as I prearranged the visitations. She insisted she be present, and I didn't mind for more selfish reasons than the well-being of my kids.

She was getting to me despite my hands-off oath, an oath I was beginning to question.

Every time I was near her, my heart raced and my body hummed. When she was gone, something was missing, and I felt empty. Hockey was the only thing that quelled the emptiness, and I was beginning to wonder if hockey had been doing that very thing for longer than I cared to admit. The breakup from my college girlfriend hadn't bothered me as much as it did when I hadn't seen Caro for a day or two. I was getting in deeper and deeper.

Our chemistry had survived the years and the secrets. When I wasn't with her or playing hockey, my thoughts centered on her and my children. Despite my intentions, I was confused and conflicted as to where Caro should fit into my life. Should she fit? Did I want her to fit? At times I did, and at others, I wanted to escape to my Puck Brother existence and pretend she wasn't anyone special, which made me either smart or delusional.

"Easton?" Caro nudged me to get my attention. "Does this work for you?"

I squinted and tried to recall what she'd said. Oh, yeah, I remembered. She wanted a specific schedule. "Nope, not during hockey season. I'm not budging on this topic."

As much as she wanted to nail down everything to specific dates and times, I refused to waver on keeping it loose during the hockey season.

She sighed. She hated backing down as much as I did. "Fine. We'll revisit everything once the season ends, and we've had time to evaluate how it's going."

"Sounds good."

Holy hockey pucks, she smelled incredible, but then she always smelled like a fresh field of wildflowers in the spring sunshine. If I didn't watch it, I'd be spouting fucking poetry.

"Easton? You're doing it again. Pay attention. You're worse than your son."

That brought a grin to my face, and Caro rolled her eyes.

"Sorry." I tried to sound contrite but didn't pull it off.

"Is that all?"

I pulled my head out of my ass and brought up the biggest elephant in the room. "Uh, no, on the matter of when to reveal I'm their father..." I hesitated. This would be one of the trickiest subjects to broach.

"They need more time. Their father's death is still fresh in their minds. Such a revelation would be too big of a shock to them this soon."

"And when will it ever be a good time?" I leaned across the table and stared pointedly at her. I read the answer in her eyes. It'd never be a good time.

"I'll play it your way for a while, but I'm not going to wait forever."

"Thank you," she conceded.

"Has it occurred to you the longer we wait, the worse it might be for them?"

She met my gaze, and I saw the worry in her blue eyes. "Yes, it's definitely occurred to me."

I didn't belabor the point. She felt bad enough about the situation. For now, I'd content myself with being the doting next-door neighbor.

"About the child support—" I pushed a check across the table to her. "My attorney felt this amount was reasonable and fair."

She picked it up, and her mouth dropped open in shock. Incredulously, she lifted her gaze back to mine and shook her head. "This is too much."

"I don't think it's enough," I countered.

"I'm already living here rent-free thanks to you. I can't accept this kind of money."

"Caro, hear me out." I grabbed both her hands in mine and squeezed them. "It's in my best interests you have enough disposable income to afford that college education you've been talking about."

"But this is too generous." A lone tear slid down her cheek. "I don't deserve your kindness. How can I ever make it up to you?"

The bad boy in me surfaced before I could muzzle him. "I could name a few things for starters." I winked at her, grinning broadly.

Sorry, not sorry that I'd thrown the sexual component out there.

"What are you saying?" She tugged on her hands, but I held tight. She glared at me, and I chuckled. Much to my surprise, she laughed. Her laughter captured my heart and locked it under her spell. Everything about her captivated me, just as it had years ago. I loved the feeling of her soft hands in my rough ones. The differences between us aroused the man inside me, and I wasn't able to hold him back this time.

"I want you," I blurted out, channeling my teenage, horny-boy self. "I can't stop thinking about you naked. I'm going crazy with lust, and I'm tired of satisfying myself when I'd much rather you satisfied me."

"You *want* me?" She sounded incredulous, which was almost as funny as my interest in her was blatantly obvious.

"I want to *fuck* you," I clarified bluntly, annoyed with myself that deep down I might want more.

"Oh." Her face fell, and sadness flashed briefly in those hypnotic eyes. She'd been hoping for something different, and I'd stomped on that seed before it had a chance to grow. This wasn't about anything but sex, damn it. As hard as it was for me to see her hurt, I had to be perfectly clear. A person didn't do what she did and expect to be forgiven. There had to be consequences to withholding a father from his children. *But she hadn't known,* said my fairer, nicer side. *Bullshit,* said the asshole in me.

"I want to bury my cock inside your warm body and slam into you until you beg me for mercy. Then I'll turn you over and finish the job from behind. Later, you can ride me, or I'll take you up against the wall. Hell, there are hundreds of ways I want to fuck you." Explaining what I wanted in graphic detail distracted me from what I really wanted—or thought I did.

"And if I say no?"

"That's your choice. The money isn't tied to having sex with me, but if things advanced beyond friends to friends with benefits, I'd welcome the change."

"You think we're friends?"

"We don't hate each other anymore. I'm working on the friends part."

"You still blame me."

"A little." I spoke honestly. "Maybe my resentment and bitterness prevent us from ever having that special thing we had before, but it doesn't stand in the way of sex. We were explosive together, and our chemistry is still there. Don't you feel it?" I'd never planned on propositioning her, especially not following a discussion about money, but I wasn't taking it back now. I made it clear where she stood with me. She had the power to say yes or no to a purely physical relationship.

She chewed on her lower lip, much like our daughter did when contemplating a decision. "I don't know."

"You don't have to give me an answer right away. After all, you know where to find me."

She nodded. Her blue eyes were troubled, and I fought off a wave of guilt at reducing our former relationship to something carnal and almost demeaning. She tugged again on my hands gripping hers, and I let go. Caro stood and walked into the kitchen. Unable to resist, I followed her and spun her around.

"You do make me crazy." I put my hands on her waist and lifted her onto the counter. Before I knew what I was doing, my mouth was on hers, hot, hungry, and demanding. Instead of pushing me away, she gave it right back to me, wrapping her legs around my waist and pushing her crotch against mine. She whimpered into my mouth, and I groaned in response. She tasted of broken promises and no-strings sex with no expectations of a future. For reasons I chose not to explore, that saddened me. I'd set the rules of this game, and I'd be bound to live by them.

I didn't know what I wanted beyond today, but I was pretty clear on the present. I needed this woman right now like a hockey player needs his skates. Okay, stupid analogy, but I wasn't a fucking poet. I was a guy in the presence of a beyond sexy woman who was offering her body to me to do with as I pleased.

She felt so fucking good, writhing against me like she was trying to rub my clothes off. I slid my hands underneath her sweater, feeling her sweet, smooth skin against my palms. I ran my fingers up her rib cage, feeling every indentation, not stopping when I touched her bra. Upward my fingers journeyed. Her bra was one of those lacy things. Her nipples were erect against the thin material. I ran my thumbs over them, and she rewarded me with a gasp of pure pleasure.

"I want to take your nipples into my mouth one at a time and suck until you are begging for mercy."

"Then do it," she challenged me, and I did love a good challenge.

If I wanted, she'd let me fuck her right here on the kitchen counter. Right now. And, damn, did I want to be inside her body again. I had to know if the sex was as epic between us as I remembered or if my mind had built it up over the years into something it wasn't.

"Let's fuck right now."

She didn't protest, so I kept kissing her, revving up the passion quotient in both of us, until I thought I'd explode. I rubbed my hard cock against her, but dry humping wasn't enough. It'd never been enough as teenagers. I needed more, and I wasn't sure how much more would satisfy my craving for her and only her.

I'd felt this same way the first night we'd met, and the chemistry between us had exploded, and there'd been no turning back. We fucked every chance we got, and right now, I felt like a horny teenage boy once again. Only she wasn't that teenage girl I'd known. She'd probably learned quite a few moves since them, and I was dying to have her try them out on me.

I yanked her sweater over her head, and she lifted her arms to help. I tossed it to the tiled floor. Her bra followed it a few seconds later. I held her at arm's length for a few seconds, allowing my hungry gaze to drink in her beautiful body. Despite having had twins, she looked fucking great. Her body wasn't the slender body of a teenager, but curvier and hotter if you asked me.

Bending my head, I slid my tongue across her nipple, pinching the other at the same time. Her breasts were bigger than I remembered, and I enjoyed every mouthful. She moaned, low and deep.

I ran my palm down her stomach to the fly on her jeans and flicked open the button. The sound of the zipper being pulled downward must have alerted her. She pushed on my chest and struggled against me. I stopped, still holding her against me. I didn't want to let her go.

"Easton," she panted against my neck, "the kids. I have to pick them up from school."

Somehow her words penetrated my foggy, lust-crazed brain. I backed a few steps away, and she skittered past me, picked up her sweater and bra, and sprinted down the hall. A few seconds later, the bathroom door slammed.

With a sigh, I glanced longingly down the hall. I debated on going after her, but doing so would only increase my frustration. The kids came first. I gathered my things and let myself out. The most I would get tonight was a cold shower, but I had my answer. There would be more times like this one, and we wouldn't stop until we were both satisfied.

I was a patient man, and I would wait for her. She was worth it.

Chapter Seventeen

ICE CREAM

--Caroline--

I avoided Junie the rest of the day, pretty sure she'd be able to guess what I'd been about to do. The next morning, Easton left on his road trip, giving me a break from having to see his handsome face.

When Junie got off work, she poured herself a glass of wine and sat next to me on the couch. The kids were curled up on the large sectional. Hailey was reading, and Heath had his Legos spread all over. I was in for a grilling, but the kids' presence made that difficult. Junie studied me as if she saw right through all the bullshit to the confused woman underneath.

I swear that woman had a hidden camera in here and knew I'd almost done the nasty with Easton on the kitchen counter yesterday. What little we did had felt so damn good and been so damn wrong.

What had I been thinking? At a time when I should have some pride and turn down his proposition, I'd done the exact opposite. He'd given me a big check, and then I'd given him a big hard-on. Regardless of whether or not he'd said the money wasn't tied to sex, I was having a hard time separating the two.

I wouldn't succumb to passion again. He'd made it clear. He didn't want a relationship. He wanted sex. He wasn't sure he even liked me.

I was pretty sure if I fucked him, I'd fall back in love with him, if I'd ever fallen out of love.

Then there were the kids to consider. I was playing a dangerous game with them and didn't know what to do to make it right. They'd lost one father, and I wouldn't allow the loss of another. I had to be one-hundred-percent certain Easton would be there for them through the good and bad times, not just when he found it convenient. Once the newness of being a father wore off, would he go back to being a guy who partied as hard as he played hockey?

I didn't want that man as the father of my children.

Of course, that ship had sailed. He was their biological father, and nothing I did would change their DNA. All I had left was to do damage control and make this transition as painless as possible for them. They'd hate me for keeping Easton a secret, but they were young, and they'd soon get over it.

"Hey, by the way, Easton left this package while you were out shopping this morning," Junie said. By her smile, she was aware of the contents.

Hailey perked up, dropped her book, and ran to me. "What did he bring?"

Heath abandoned the skyscraper he was building with Legos and joined us. He was almost smiling in anticipation. His hopeful expression was heartening to see.

I glanced at Junie, and she nodded, reading my mind. Whatever was in here was okay to open in front of the kids. After yesterday, I'd almost expected a sexy negligée and was stupidly disappointed the gift wasn't going to be that intimate.

"Why don't you open it?" I handed the package to Heath. Hailey bounced on the balls of her feet. Unable to contain her excitement, she tore at the packaging, while Heath batted at her hands.

Finally, the thing was open, and several Sockeyes jerseys fell to the floor, followed by an envelope. The kids ignored the envelope and rifled through the jerseys, finding the one that fit them. They tugged them on. Hailey danced around the room, pretending she was figure skating. Heath slid across the hardwood floor shooting an imaginary puck into the kitchen and racing after it. I hadn't seen him this animated in a long while. Both jerseys had Black on the back and Easton's number.

There were two more Black jerseys presumably for Junie and me.

"Open the envelope," Junie prodded, as giddy as the kids.

I picked it up and tore open the flap to find four hockey tickets to next Saturday's game.

"I guess we're going to the game on Saturday," Junie said.

I opened my mouth to protest on principle only. The kids didn't know Easton played hockey, and I'd been stalling because he'd be even more of a hero in their eyes once they found out. They'd taken to Easton in ways I'd only imagined, and I'd been feeling left out and sorry for myself. Easton was the shiny new toy, and I was the dependable, old stuffed animal they'd turn to when things went sideways.

"We're going," Junie insisted, shutting down my excuses before I had a chance to fully formulate them. "We can't pass on this opportunity, any more than I can pass on what's in this building."

"This building?"

"Yeah, here. Duh. We live in a building that's a smorgasbord of hot hockey players, and I can't decide which one to eat next." Junie shot me a wicked grin.

"Have you already sampled any of them?" I lowered my voice, but the kids weren't paying us any attention. Heath was weaving in and out of the chairs and circling his sister, while she did her figure skating routine across the hardwood floor and sang her own version of a Disney song.

"Not yet, but I'm working on it. Several have offered to be my next meal."

I rolled my eyes. "Junie, you're disgusting."

"I'm having fun. You should do the same, or have you already sampled what Easton has to offer?"

"Of course not. We're barely friends." I was pretty sure my face gave away my bald-faced lie because Junie laughed.

"It's okay. You can have sex with him. He's hot and available. You don't have to have a committed relationship with every guy you hook up with. Learn to be more casual about sex. You're so rigid."

"I am not," I protested, refusing to see the truth in her statement.

"Kids!" shouted Junie, "we're going to the hockey game on Saturday."

The kids cheered and gathered around us. I hugged them both.

Yes, we were going to a hockey game.

As for sex with Easton...

--Caroline--

Saturday evening, loaded down with junk food and dressed in our jerseys, we navigated down the stadium stairs and found our seats on the glass. Junie sat on one side of me, while the kids sat on the other.

I hadn't seen Easton since we'd discussed the visitation plan. The team had flown into Seattle early Friday morning, and, yes, I knew his schedule. He hadn't checked in, not that I expected him to do so, or had I? I might even be a little disappointed that he hadn't bothered to drop in last night to check on the kids—his kids.

As we took our seats, the team skated onto the ice for warm-ups. I spotted Easton immediately. I'd recognize the way he moved anywhere, even under his uniform and padding. He moved with energy combined with coordination, overtly masculine in his grace. He owned the ice, commanded it, made it conform to his wishes, and he was a joy to watch.

Junie elbowed me and smirked. "You're drooling all over your new jersey."

"I am not."

Junie snorted so hard she almost sucked beer up her nose. "Whatever."

I ignored her. Right now, my eyes were on Easton and Easton only.

I didn't care that Junie was witnessing my pathetic crush on a hot hockey player, if that's what this was.

Easton turned away from a drill he'd been doing when our eyes met. A slow, sexy smile lifted up both corners of his mouth and my spirits. He was happy to see me, not just the kids, but me. I warned my tender heart not to read too much into a simple smile.

Easton lazily made a circle around the boards, eventually passing us. His movements were loose and easy. He tapped on the glass with his stick as he skated past.

Hailey's eyes grew big as she realized who he was. "Mom, that was Easton. Easton is a hockey player. Did you know that? Did you know Mr. E is a hockey player? Did you? Did you? I wonder if he'll sign our jerseys. Oh. Oh. This is his number. Look, Mom, this is his number!" Hailey bounced in her seat, pointing at the number on her chest.

"Yes, I did. I—" My words were lost in the jabbering of my daughter. She was too wound up to listen. I turned to Heath, who rolled his eyes, and I had to laugh. He was coming out of his grief and turning back into the son I knew. I'd been so worried he might actually never be that happy-go-lucky kid again.

"I knew who he was all along. He's Big E," Heath said with a superior smirk. Even Hailey stopped her constant stream of words to gape at him.

"You did not," Hailey and I both said at the same time.

He shrugged and didn't say any more. Every time Easton came to the condo, Heath had stared at him with hero worship in his brown eyes. Maybe he had known all along but been afraid to say anything. Easton would get a kick out of this. Next time I saw him, I'd be sure to tell him that Heath had rendered Hailey speechless.

My daughter shrugged, already bored with our conversation, and leapt to her feet. She pounded on the glass with her little fists, shouting Easton's name. "Easton! Easton! Easton!"

I guess Hailey didn't need an answer or explanation as to why I hadn't told them Easton played hockey. One obstacle crossed with minor damage. I let out a sigh of relief.

Heath shot up next to her and pounded on the glass too. He didn't shout Easton's name, but he was smiling broadly, as if this was his best day ever. Their excitement warmed my insides. Easton had done the right thing by them, even though I'd had my doubts. Maybe he did have some fathering instincts, and maybe I was too overprotective and worried too much.

Easton skated by again and casually tossed a hockey puck over the glass. Heath caught it and held it up for us to see. His grin spread wider than before.

Hailey jumped up and down and pounded even harder, wanting her own puck. Easton did a slow, lazy circle and tossed another. Hailey missed it, but I caught it and handed it to her. She fist-bumped Heath and erupted into another steady string of chattering, talking so fast I had a hard time understanding her. Nothing unusual there. She was talking to her brother anyway, so I turned away and took a sip of the beer I'd bought earlier. I never really knew if Heath understood her because of some twin-bond thing they had going or if he only pretended to do so.

I glanced at Junie. Her eyes were glued to the ice. I followed her gaze in an attempt to figure out what guy she was so zeroed-in on. Could it be Kaden who was the current subject of Junie's attention? Or would that be the current victim she was stalking? Hard to tell with Junie, but she never led guys on. She was in it for sex, fun, and nothing long-term. These hot hockey players were right up her alley and prime game. I was surprised she hadn't hooked up with any of them yet, but maybe she was taking her time and savoring the hunt.

My attention strayed back to Easton. He was all business now, concentrating on scoring drills with the two other guys on his line. He moved with the speed and precision of a trained athlete, a man who'd taken advantage of his innate physical ability and honed his body and mind to reach the highest level of his chosen sport. Easton was good, really good, and I was proud of him even if I didn't have the right to be.

For a long time, I'd resented hockey, blamed the sport for ripping him away from me. Now I saw things as they were. If we'd stayed together back then, we wouldn't have lasted. We were too young with too many strikes against us. Young love burned hot and fast but often didn't have staying power as the couple matured and grew in different and opposing directions.

Easton might have been the love of my teenage life, but I'd find the right man, one who made time for me and the kids rather than disappearing for a week at a time on a road trip, one who wasn't surrounded by women who'd do anything to hook up with a hockey player, one who didn't live in the limelight and take advantage of the fame.

I wanted a quiet life. I didn't want to be in the spotlight, nor did I want my kids subjected to life under a microscope. I made a mental note to have a discussion with Easton about his public life versus our private life and what we'd do to protect the kids.

I sighed and rubbed my eyes, suddenly weary. I had a predatory female on the right side of me and, on the other side, two kids who hero-worshipped a man they didn't know was their father. Here I was, struggling against an insane attraction to Easton that collided with my unreasonable jealousy toward my kids' growing attachment to him. Even worse, thoughts of him invaded my mind all day and night long. When sleep finally claimed me, my subconscious didn't give me a break, either, and conjured up erotic dreams of things I wanted to do to him—hot, dirty things, the dirtier the better.

I was a hot mess and miring myself deeper in the muck every minute of every day.

Easton's insanely generous check sat in my bank account barely touched. I was afraid to spend it for fear it'd go more quickly than planned. Next week, I'd register for classes at a local college, thereby cementing my commitment to living in this area for the next few years. Later, I'd go Christmas shopping and probably spend too much money making this first Christmas without Mark a good one for the kids.

I wasn't sure I'd succeed, but I'd do my best.

Mark had loved Christmas. Every year we'd picked out a tree and decorated it as a family. This year, I'd continue some of Mark's family traditions and add a few of my own. We'd create new memories and honor the old ones, and we'd find our new normal.

I'd adjust to Easton's presence in my life, as I both hoped and feared he was here to stay—because of the children, of course.

It'd been years since I'd seen hockey played live, and live hockey was so much better than hockey on television. I gave up trying to follow the game and resigned myself to my obsession with Easton. My hungry eyes ate him up, watching his every move when he was on the ice and on the bench. I marveled at the power in his legs and the speed with which he skated from one end of the ice to the other, not to mention the skill he exhibited handling the puck. He'd been good back in his teens, but he was far beyond good now. He was exceptional in an arena filled with exceptional athletes at the top of their game.

I'd stalked him online. The sports bloggers and online websites touted him as one of the most talented rookies of the season. I easily saw why. He stood out. He made plays. He was dependable and steady, yet unpredictable and dangerous to the opposing team.

My kids were enamored of him, and I was conflicted. I didn't want to like him, yet I did. I didn't want to be attracted to him, yet I was. I didn't want to love him, yet it might be too late.

--Easton--

Having my children and the mother of those children watch me playing hockey had a profound effect on me. I hadn't realized how emotional I'd be until I saw those kids' faces pressed against the glass as they shouted at me to get my attention.

I choked up, my eyes burned with unshed tears, and I fought to hold these emotions overwhelming me in check. They looked great in my jerseys, and several teammates approached me at the intermission to shake my hand and congratulate me on being a father. Better late than never, but as soon as it could be given the circumstances.

The word sped through the team faster than a puck sped to the net. Once a few of my buddies knew, all the coaches and staff knew. Cousin Coop wanted to meet everyone, and I promised we'd arrange that soon and begged him not to tell my family. I wanted to tell them in person.

Then there was Caro. One look at her in my hockey jersey, and I wanted to stamp my name all over her. Jealousy clawed my insides knowing she and my kids had someone else's last name. I planned on rectifying the twins' last name as soon as they knew about me. As far as Caro was concerned, the only way to change her name would be to marry her.

Marriage was something I'd always imagined I'd do far into the future when I found the right woman. Caro might be the woman I wanted to fuck, but I didn't know where we'd end up beyond that, and I didn't want to think about such things.

Better to focus on today. Enjoy my twenties. Party while I could. Be the best dad when I could. And stay away from long-term relationships with any woman. I was too young to know what I wanted out of life, including the woman I wanted. In my opinion, I'd only get one chance to do this right. When I married, I'd marry for life. I suppose everyone thought they would, but I was determined to make my marriage last, just as I'd been determined to be a professional hockey player. Failure wasn't an option.

After the game, Caro took the kids home. Junie and I went to the after-game party, but my heart wasn't in it. When Kaden offered to give Junie a ride home later, I had zero reason to stick around.

Instead of going to my condo, I stopped at a grocery store and made a purchase. Once home, I hesitated at my door, crossed the hall, and listened at Caro's door like some kind of sick stalker. When I heard the television, I knocked lightly. I wiped my palms on my dress pants and ran my fingers through my hair. Plastering a pleasant smile on my face, I waited.

A few seconds later, the door opened. Caro stood there, dressed in sweats and a hoodie, with fuzzy slippers on her feet. Her luxurious hair was tied up in a ponytail, and her skin was devoid of makeup. She looked sexier than any model I'd ever taken to a black-tie affair.

"Easton, what are you doing here?"

Knowing her weakness, I held up a carton of Ben and Jerry Chocolate Fudge Brownie ice cream.

She clapped her hands together in child-like glee. "You remembered."

I remembered, all right. I remembered smearing it all over her body, even the more intimate parts, and licking it off. My dick responded with a hell yeah, ready for a repeat of that seven-year-old performance.

Her face flushed when she realized what I was actually remembering.

"I mean you remembered how much I loved this. I mean, love this ice cream. I mean, I—" She was stammering and stuttering and had the most adorable flushed face.

I pushed past her into the living room, not allowing her to protest. I paused to appreciate the little touches she'd added to the once-sterile décor to warm it up and make it a home. I'd have to ask her to do the same for my place.

"Where are the kids?"

"In bed. They were exhausted. It'd take a stampede of elephants to wake them."

"Good." I didn't comment further as my filthy mind turned down a dirty path. This might be an even better night than planned. Maybe I'd put that ice cream to good use after all.

I rummaged in a couple kitchen drawers and produced two spoons, then plopped down on the couch. I patted the cushion next to me. Caro hesitated, but when I held the first spoonful of ice cream up to my lips and made a show of sucking it into my mouth, she laughed.

Caro sat down next to me, keeping a safe distance between us. Safe was an illusion. I was anything but safe tonight. I wanted her. I'd had a taste of her earlier this week, and I craved more of the same and then some.

She reached for a spoon and dug in. I watched as she put the spoon to her lips and licked the ice cream off it. Oh, fuck. I was going to lose it just watching her. A dab of ice cream was on her lower lip. Before she wiped it off, I leaned in and slid my tongue along her lips, savoring the sweetness of the ice cream combined with the heady taste of her.

My cock jerked in my dress pants, begging to do the deed. My boy was tired of being told no, and to be honest, so was I.

Caro pushed me away. Her eyes were wide and questioning as she gazed up at me. When she looked at me like that, I wanted to be her hero, but I wasn't anyone's hero, and that line of thinking was going to get me in deep shit.

"Don't push me away. You want this as much as I do."

"The kids," she countered in a hushed tone with a glance over her shoulder toward the long hallway.

"You said yourself it'd take a stampede of elephants to wake them."

"I'm not ready."

"You feel ready to me." I ran my hand over her crotch.

She sucked in a deep breath and gazed up at me with glazed eyes. She was unable to resist me. I saw the lust peppered with resignation in her eyes, as if she'd given up fighting me.

Resignation?

That wasn't what I wanted from her. Right then, I knew the time wasn't right. I couldn't do this, not under these circumstances, and I hated myself for being so noble.

I scooted away and rose to my feet.

Chapter Eighteen

NOT RUSHING

--Caroline--

blinked several times, attempting to get my bearings. One second, Easton and I were on the verge of fucking each other's brains out; the next, he stood away from me, hands in his pockets, while his impressive erection pushed against the fly of his pants.

Stunned by what just happened and trying to make sense of his actions, I stared dumbly at his crotch for a long time before dragging my gaze up his body to his face.

"Easton?"

"I can't do this." He was in agony yet determined.

"What?" I stared at him incredulously, not making sense of his words.

"It's the look on your face."

"What look?"

"I saw the look on your face, like you were resigned to your fate. I don't want sex with you to be like that. Either we're both looking forward to fucking with zero regrets or we aren't doing it. I don't want to hurt you or be hurt by you. I don't want resignation. I want what we used to have—fire, passion, absolute commitment to each other's pleasure."

"I'm confused." Easton just turned me down, and I was shocked.

"You're the mother of my children. I can't walk away and never see you again. We're forever bound together by the twins. Therefore, we need an amicable relationship. If sex causes you regrets, we can't do it. We have to be on the same page and want this for the same reasons."

"And those reasons are?"

"Short term, sexual gratification and fun. Long term, I haven't a fucking clue."

At least he was honest.

"We're on the same page," I said quietly.

"I don't think so."

I considered protesting but didn't and nodded slowly. "I understand."

"I'm leaving it up to you. I want you, Caro, so badly I haven't looked at another woman since you came back in my life, but any relationship beyond friends causes complications. Are you willing to live with those complications? I know we have to think of the kids. You plan everything. Maybe you need to figure out if sex with me fits in your plan."

He was right, and there wasn't any arguing with his logic.

"I'll think on it."

Easton's longing gaze did nothing to sooth the turmoil boiling inside me. With a wry smile, he walked to the apartment door and let himself out.

I wanted him, but he'd made it clear he didn't want emotional attachments. Would I be able to do that?

Yes, I told myself, I would. I'd experienced the white picket fence with two kids and a husband. Been there, done that. My priorities were different now. I needed security for my children and me, but I'd work toward independence and not lean on a man for anything. I wouldn't be my mother, who'd required a man to bring home a paycheck and never picked the right man. She'd also considered her children inconveniences and done minimal parenting. She dumped me off with my older sister, who was struggling in her own living hell married to an abuser.

My senior year, I'd started dating Mark. His family had been my first taste of normal. Like a drug, I'd craved more normalcy. I'd clung to him like a lifeline until he'd left that summer for a tour of Europe, and I'd met Easton. We'd had a magical summer, but magic usually ended and you were left with nothing.

Now I had to save myself. I'd enroll in the winter quarter at the local college, and I'd never depend on a man for the basic necessities of life again.

Sleeping with Easton for pure enjoyment would prove I was nobody's fool. I was a strong, independent woman who made mature decisions and was able to separate emotion from recreation.

I could do this.

--Easton--

After leaving Caro's, I trudged across the hall to my condo and let myself in. Steele was sprawled on the sectional watching a whodunnit, his jam as much as the Food Channel was Kaden's.

"Hey," I said as I slumped next to him.

"Hey," he said back, never taking his eyes off the TV.

"Where's Kaden?"

Steele shrugged. "Where's Junie? He was supposed to bring her home."

"Oh, she's doing shots with some of the guys. One of them will see that she gets home."

"You don't know where Kaden is?"

"Probably with his secret girlfriend. Don't think he'll be home tonight."

"The one we think is married?"

"Yeah, the one he's texting all the time. The one he sneaks off to meet. She has to be married. They never come here or go to her place. They get a hotel room."

"How do you know this shit?"

"I listen."

"Eavesdrop," I corrected.

"Not on purpose, but the two of you aren't exactly discreet."

"Why are you including me in this?"

"Because you have the hots for the mother of your children."

"I do not."

"You were strutting around like a bantam rooster when you saw Caro and the kids sitting behind the glass wearing your jerseys."

"I was not." I sounded like a whiny little boy who'd gotten caught filling up on candy before dinner.

Steele snorted and rolled his eyes. "You're a dweeb."

"A dweeb?"

"Yeah, in denial and too stupid to see what you want and go after it. Life is like hockey. If you want the big payout, you have to work for it." Steele shrugged. This was the most I'd ever heard him say.

"Like you do?" The guy seldom dated or hooked up. He was a loner who rarely let anyone see even a glimpse of what was going on in his head. He was a great roommate. Quiet, no drama, and anal about housekeeping—one of us had to be.

Instead of being offended, he cracked a rare grin. "Yeah, like me."

I grinned back at him. "Sometimes life isn't as cut and dried as hockey. I mean, in hockey, there are definite rungs in the ladder, the top two being making the NHL and winning the Cup. In life, it's not so obvious."

"Why don't you just tell her you're crazy about her and figure out if you can start a life together. Then the remaining Puck Brothers can decide on a punishment."

"I'm not crazy about her, so don't start coming up with shit. There's no reason to rush into anything."

"But you're rushing." His smugness was starting to piss me off.

"I am not. She's recovering from the death of her husband. That takes time, and I don't want to be the rebound relationship. That shit never lasts. I wouldn't be averse to sex. I had some of the best sex of my life when I was with her."

"Did you ever stop to think it was so good because there was more to it than sex?" Steele shot me an unreadable look, stood, and left the room. I heard his bedroom door click shut a few seconds later.

I stared out the huge windows at the night sky and pondered what he'd said. Sometimes Steele was wise beyond his years.

Chapter Nineteen

UP TO THE TASK

--Caroline--

he next three weeks sped by. Easton was a constant presence in our condo when he wasn't on a road trip. Somehow, we'd managed to keep our clothes on thanks to one long road trip and two kids who constantly demanded his attention. Regardless, he sent sizzling looks my way often, and I lobbed them right back, and we did manage to steal a few hot kisses in the hallway between condos.

Moving here just before the holidays hadn't been one of my smarter plans. I was running on empty. Not only had I spent the last few weeks unpacking and putting away everything, but I'd spent the better part of the day decorating for Christmas. Tomorrow was Christmas Eve, and I was ill-prepared for the holiday. I hadn't made my usual lists, but Hailey had done me proud. She had a list a mile long. Heath only wanted one thing, the very thing his father had promised him but would never be able to give him. I'd found the next best thing, and I prayed he'd see it as an acceptable replacement.

Thank God for Junie. She'd taken the kids to see Santa this morning so I'd be able to work without interruption.

Sadly, Christmas had been an afterthought this year with everything else going on. The kids vacillated between excitement and sadness. This was their first Christmas without Mark and their grandparents, and their absence would be hard on them. It was hard on me. I'd invited Fran and Howard to visit for Christmas, but they'd just settled into their Arizona home. They promised we'd spend the next Christmas together.

Mark and I had our family Christmas traditions, such as decorating the tree together. I'd order pizza, and Fran would bring chocolate cheesecake and eggnog. Mark and his father put the lights on the tree. The kids added the ornaments where they could reach. Mark placed the tree topper on the tree. We turned off all the lamps, and Mark made a big production of turning on the tree lights. We called it the Mills' tree-lighting ceremony. Later, Mark and I would shoo the kids off to bed, put presents under the tree, and fill their stockings amid sips of eggnog and laughter.

I lived in my own personal snow globe, where everything was perfect and nothing from the outside could get in. All the signs had been there—Mark's late nights, disinterest in sex, and bored responses with me. We'd stopped discussing our future and having date nights. We'd fallen into a rut. We were comfortable, and all my attempts to spice up our marriage and elicit a response from him had failed miserably.

I'd depended on a man for my happiness, my financial stability, and my self-esteem. I'd stand on my own two feet and be strong for myself and my children.

Right now, that strength required I lift my weary body off this couch and continue with the Christmas decorations. I still hadn't purchased a tree. I'd been miserly with the money I'd received from Easton, but I hadn't considered the hundreds of dollars I spent on decorations. Christmas decorations were expensive when you were starting at ground zero. Even my careful list making hadn't been foolproof, and I'd forgotten several essential items.

Someone rang the doorbell, and I dragged my weary body to the

door. I checked the peephole and saw Easton's beaming face. With a
sigh, I opened the door and jumped backward. The huge evergreen
tree dwarfed the rather large hallway.

"Hey, where would you like this?" Easton asked.

"I...uh...I..." Unable to respond, I merely stood back and allowed
Steele and Easton to wrestle the large tree past me. I followed them
into the living room, where Easton positioned the tree next to the
corner by the large wall of windows.

"What do you think?" he said.

"I'm overwhelmed. It's beautiful, but I don't have a tree stand."

"We have all that." As if on cue, another knock sounded on the
door. I opened it find to a stack of boxes, behind which was Kaden. He
carefully entered the apartment with the boxes tottering precariously. I
held on to the top one to balance them until he put them down.

The three guys grinned at each other, pleased with themselves.

"Merry Christmas." Kaden swept low in a bow, gracing me with one
of his charming grins.

Steele cast a rare grin in my direction.

"From our condo to yours," Easton added. His eyes lit up like the
lights on a Christmas tree. He was getting a kick out of this. "Where
are the twins?"

"Junie took them with her for some last-minute shopping."

"Let's get this set up before they arrive home." Easton rummaged
through the stack of boxes until he found the Christmas tree stand. I'd
never had a real tree. Mark and I had a pre-lit artificial tree. It'd looked
like the real deal but didn't spread needles all over or need to be
watered. I glanced downward in disdain at the trail of needles across
my clean carpet.

Easton could've asked first. I didn't like being surprised. I'd had a
plan, and now he'd messed up my plan. He was becoming quite
talented at that.

Regardless, I was being ungrateful, and I didn't like being that
person.

--Easton--

If I'd been decorating the tree, I'd string the lights wherever, not really caring how they looked, just getting the job done quickly. Not Caro. Every light had to be perfectly placed the same distance apart and uniform rather than concentrated in one place and sparse in another.

It was just a fucking Christmas tree.

My buddies retreated to our condo, not interested in anal Christmas tree decorating.

"Easton, the top left side, right there, the lights are in a big glob." Caro pointed upward, and I sighed.

I squinted to see what she was seeing. Looked fine to me. I stood on the stepstool and moved the lights around.

"You made it worse."

I glanced at Caro over my shoulder. She stood several feet away, hands on hips, chewing on her lower lip as she cocked her head to view the tree at a different angle. Fuck, she was hot in her red sweater and worn jeans. My annoyance gave way to desire. I lost my concentration. Arms flailing, I fought to keep my balance on top of the short ladder.

Caro giggled. "Are you okay?" she said between bouts of laughter.

"I'm fine."

"It's a good thing you skate better than you stand on a ladder." She covered her mouth with her hand, still snickering.

The uncontrollable urge to wipe that smile off her face overcame me. I scrambled down the ladder and stalked toward her, my intent clear in every determined step I took. She backed up, laughing harder. I gave chase, and she sprinted around the kitchen island. I lunged for her. She eluded me, keeping the counter between us.

For a long moment, we froze, regarding each other, the hunter and the prey. Her chest was heaving, drawing my eyes to her delectable set of tits. I didn't know of one other woman who made me feel so many things, so intently, and so deeply.

"Fuck," I whispered. Her nostrils flared and those beautiful eyes lit up. She lifted her chin slightly in a silent challenge, and I didn't wait one second longer. She wasn't getting away from me. I was a professional hockey player, a finely tuned athlete at the top of my game, a man with one thing on his mind. And that happened to be Caro.

I bolted around the counter; she raced to the other side. I faked a lunge in one direction. She dashed the other way, and I reversed direction, catching her off guard.

She squealed, attempted to spin, but she wasn't going anywhere. I wrapped my arms around her, pinned her against the counter, and brought my mouth down on hers before she had time to react. She pushed against my chest but abandoned her struggle a heartbeat later. She melted into me. Her mouth, her tongue, her lips claimed me, as I was claiming her.

Caro's fingers curled into fists in the shirt fabric at my shoulders, and she leaned harder into me, kissing me like a woman who'd been sexually starved for too long. That made two of us.

I slid my hands down her waist and cupped her gorgeous ass in my palms, pulling her even closer, letting her feel the hardness under my jeans. She made the cutest sounds as she ground her hips into mine. She was fucking driving me insane.

I was going to strip her naked and bend her over the arm of the couch. I'd thrust into her like a man possessed.

She was breathing hard as she dragged her mouth away from mine. I protested and captured her lips once again only to have her elude me once me.

"The...kids..." she said in raspy voice.

I didn't understand her words at first. They sank in slowly.

"How much—how much time do we have?" I panted against her neck.

"They'll be back any second." Her answer was robotic, her eyes glazed.

As if they'd been waiting for their cue off-stage, we heard the pounding of feet running down the hallway from the elevator.

"Fuck," I groaned, gripping her ass tighter. I didn't want to end what we'd started.

"Perfect timing." She pushed on my chest again, and this time I released her.

"Yeah, perfect." I backed away and leaned down to pick up a box of decorations, feigning interest in their contents, but I had the boner of all boners, and my boy wanted satisfaction. So did I. We were screwed, and not in a good way.

The door slammed open and hit the wall with a bang. Two whirlwinds stormed into the living room and slid to a halt in front of the large tree. They stared up at it in awe.

"We got a tree. It's really tall. Can we decorate it now? Is it real? Where's our star from our old house?" Hailey rapid-fired the questions at no one in particular.

Heath glowered at me, almost accusatorily.

"Is something wrong?" Caro asked.

"The lights are on. They shouldn't be on until we do the tree lighting." His voice dripped with disappointment and anger. I blinked a few times, not expecting such hostility and still recovering from raging lust.

Having more experience, Caro recovered faster and rushed forward. "Oh, honey, sorry, we were testing them. I'll turn them off until we do the official tree lighting tonight." Before she had a chance to unplug the lights, Heath stomped from the room. A second later, his door slammed shut. Hard.

Caro, Junie, and I exchanged glances. What had just happened? I was missing some big piece of Christmas past. Hailey ignored Heath's outburst and rummaged through the decorations.

"I apologize for his behavior. Things have been going so well, he was due for a meltdown. His dad used to make a big ceremony out of lighting our tree every year. He's struggling with change."

I nodded. My heart pinched when Caro referred to Mark as Heath's dad. I wanted to be his dad, and I'd assume that role as soon as feasibly possible. I'd tread lightly and be sensitive to the loss of the only dad they'd known. While he might not have been the best husband to Caro, by all accounts, he'd been a great father and tough act to follow.

I hoped I was up to the task, in more ways than one.

Chapter Twenty

IN MOTION

--Easton--

*T*ail tucked between my legs and my dick aching from dissatisfaction, I trudged back to my condo. I had lots to do, considering it was Christmas Eve, and I'd procrastinated as usual. Pushing thoughts of Caro and the kids from my mind, I started on my list.

I'd intended to tell my family about the twins in person, but there never seemed to be a time that worked out for all of us to be together. My two brothers played for hockey teams in different parts of the country. My hardworking mother, our rock, had decided to go on a European cruise with her single female friends for the holidays.

Since my entire team knew, it was only a matter of time before the word spread and my family found out from people other than myself. I had to tell them now, before that happened. Mom was in port and was calling at one p.m. I waited for her call, anxious to reveal my secret, pacing the floor as I played over and over in my mind exactly how I'd break my news to her.

Typical of Mom, the phone rang exactly at one.

"Hi, Merry Christmas, Mom," I said huskily, unable to cover up my nervousness.

"Merry Christmas, honey. Are you okay?" Her voice was laced with concern, and I cringed. She'd picked up on my tone immediately. I'd never been able to fake her out. She always knew when something was up with me or one of my brothers.

"I'm good, Mom. Really good."

"Then what's wrong?"

I closed my eyes for a moment, taking deep, calming breaths. There was nothing to be worried about. My mother would embrace having grandchildren with the same enthusiasm she attacked everything in her life.

"I have something to tell you."

"Easton, are you okay? Are your brothers okay?" She sounded alarmed, and I rushed to squelch her concerns.

"It's nothing like that. We're all fine."

"Then what is it?"

"Are you sitting down?"

"Yes."

There was no easy way to say this, so I blurted it out. "I'm a father."

I heard a gasp, after which all was quiet, so I continued.

"I found out recently that I have twins, a boy and a girl." There, I said it, got it over with, and now I waited nervously for her reaction. The phone was silent for so long I thought we'd been disconnected. "Mom? You still there?"

"Yes," she answered shakily. "I'm processing. Would you care to elaborate?"

I told her everything about Caro, about the death of her husband, about the kids, and about her moving to Seattle. She listened quietly, making a brief comment here and there. When I finished, I waited for her response.

"I'm surprised. I'm thrilled. I'm going to need some time to adjust to being a grandmother, but I promise you I'll be the best grandmother ever.

"I'm certain you will. I don't know how long it'll be before we reveal I'm their father, but as soon as we do, I want you to meet them."

"I can't wait, Easton. I really can't."

"They're great kids but still reeling over the death of the man they thought was their father. That's why we have to be careful about everything. They need time to heal and adjust before we drop another bombshell on them." I was parroting Caro's words, but as much as I hated to admit it, they were good words.

"And you and Caro? How is that going?" Leave it to Mom to get right down to one of the most troubling pieces of this entire mess.

"I was angry at first because I couldn't understand how she didn't know they were my children, but I'm working past that. I didn't leave her much room when I dumped her. I made it clear we were through, that I was moving on to college and the pros, and she was moving on to nursing school. She went back to her former boyfriend on the rebound and got pregnant. I guess she never imagined I was the father."

"I'm glad you're over blaming her. Time to look forward, not backward, for the children's sakes. How do you feel about her now?"

"That's the problem, Mom. I'm conflicted. I expected I'd find the same thing again with other women I dated, but I didn't. I thought once I made the NHL, I'd have arrived, and this emptiness inside of me would be gone. Pro hockey should've filled in the missing part of me, but it hasn't. I don't know if we have a future, but I wouldn't throw out the idea either."

"I've always liked Caro. Maybe she's your special someone." Mom was a bit of a romantic. After Dad had died, she'd never shown any interest in dating anyone else. My brothers and I encouraged her, but she said she was happy with her life and her friends.

"Like Dad was yours?"

"Yes, like your father was mine. I'll never have what I had with him, and I'm not looking for a replacement."

"I know, you've said that. But don't you get lonely?"

"At times, but let's not talk about me. Let's talk about you. Easton, follow your heart. What is it saying to you?"

"A couple years ago, I decided to find Caro for reasons I really couldn't explain. When I tracked her down, I sat outside her house and a guy came out along with her and the two kids. I left, feeling I'd been robbed of my life that could've been. He had the family I didn't know I wanted, and the woman I'd walked away from. Now I wonder... I'm getting a second chance. I don't know if I should take it or not." I was being brutally honest with her and with myself for the first time regarding this situation.

"Things happen for a reason. At sixteen, you weren't equipped to handle a wife and two small children. Chances are things wouldn't have worked out. Now you have another opportunity. Most people don't get that lucky."

"A do-over?" I chuckled.

"Yes, a do-over. Don't let something special slip out of your hands, Easton."

"What should I do? Should I tell her I want to give us a chance as a family? I've made a point of telling her that I don't want a relationship, just sex." I couldn't believe I was talking to my mom about stuff like this, but I had to talk to someone. Was that what I really wanted? Another chance at a relationship? Or was it the need for sex with her that was clouding my judgment? Fuck, I was confused.

"Maybe you should tell her you've changed your mind. Be honest with her and, most of all, yourself."

"I'll give it some thought."

"I have faith in you to do the right thing for everyone concerned."

"Thanks, Mom." Yeah, once I figured out what that was.

We talked a few more minutes about family stuff and ended the call. Then I phoned my two brothers and broke the news to them. They were equal parts surprised and thrilled to have a niece and nephew. Of course, they gave me all manners of shit for getting a girl pregnant in the first place. I wouldn't have expected any less of them.

After I ended the last call, I sat in silence, trying to process what to do next. If I was Caro, I'd make a list, but I wasn't Caro. I tended to dive in and think about the consequences later.

Did I want just sex, or did I want more? Maybe testing the waters with every possibility on the table would be the best way to go.

But first...

I'd put off Christmas shopping until the last minute, typical of me, but now I knew what I needed to buy and had very little time to do it. I made a few phone calls and set everything in motion.

This would be a Christmas to remember.

Chapter Twenty-One

EGGNOG TOASTS

--Easton--

*A*fter I finished shopping, I drove out of Seattle to the burbs where Ice and Avery lived. Our captain had invited the entire team to an open house on Christmas Eve, and I felt obligated to put in an appearance. Ice was a private person who was trying to come out of his shell, and I appreciated this gesture.

As a rookie, I was always trying to make a good impression on my veteran teammates and my coaches. As much as I'd preferred to insinuate myself into Caro's evening, attending this party was necessary.

I double-checked the address multiple times as I drove farther into the country. I had Ice pegged as a city boy, and living out here didn't fit with my image of him. My GPS told me to turn down a narrow gravel lane lined with trees and a white-rail fence. In the distance were a couple large barns. I drove past the barns and turned down another driveway. As the thick trees opened up, a large two-story home lit up with Christmas lights came into view. I was surprised once again as I pictured Ice on a ladder stringing lights from his eaves.

His driveway was clogged with cars, and I pulled behind Steele's car, surprised to see my roommate was already present.

I grabbed the gift bag containing a nice bottle of wine from the seat beside me and stepped out of my truck. The evening was clear and brisk, a nice respite from the incessant rain and gray skies of the past few weeks.

Several of my teammates stood on the front porch flanking the entire front of the farmhouse. They were drinking beers and laughing. I walked onto the porch and greeted everyone, stood outside for a short time, and ventured in the house to find my host and hostess.

Avery and Ice stood in the large living room with a huge rock fireplace on one wall, talking to Smooth and his wife, Bella, along with Brick and Amelia.

"Hey, glad you could make it." Ice was beaming from ear to ear. Glancing down at Avery's stomach, I could see why. She wasn't showing a lot yet, but her pregnancy was obvious. Not to mention, Avery inadvertently called attention to her baby bump by rubbing her stomach quite often.

I shook hands with the guys and hugged the women, then settled back into conversation that ran the gamut from hockey to kids to buying a house. I didn't say much, just listened and observed. The three couples were very much in love. They were always touching, sharing private glances, and standing close to each other. Bella liked to finish Smooth's sentences, but he didn't seem to mind. Amelia often directed the convo to kids, while Avery often talked about horses. Every one of them gave me advice on being a dad, and I discussed riding lessons for my daughter with Avery.

Eventually, the couples wandered off to mingle, and Avery excused herself to check on the caterers.

"How are you, Big E?" Ice asked when we had a rare moment alone. To my surprise, his blue eyes were warm and inviting.

"I'm doing okay. I'm spending the day tomorrow with the kids and Caro."

"How's that going with Caro?" He seemed genuinely interested.

"I don't know. I don't think either of us can figure out what we want—friends, physical, or an actual relationship."

Ice chucked. "Been there. Honestly, love will bite you in the ass before you even realize what's happening. I sure as fuck wasn't looking for the love of my life when I met Avery, but I didn't have the strength to resist."

"I don't either."

He nodded sagely and rubbed his chin. He was sporting a beard this season though he kept it trimmed short. "You can't stop love, buddy. If you're in love with someone, no amount of resistance will work, and just the dumb-ass, moony expression on your face when you talk about her tells me all I need to know."

Moony was a word I'd never expected to hear from Ice's lips. "You think I look like that?"

"Fuck yeah. It's obvious to everyone but you. That's the way it is with guys who think they're in control when they're not."

"Everyone?" I was horrified. I didn't want my heart on my sleeve when I hadn't even acknowledged my emotions in my most private of thoughts.

"What's the worst thing that could happen if you and she give it a try?"

"I don't know. We might break up."

"Is that worse than not trying, never knowing, and always regretting?"

I shrugged.

"It's like not taking a shot when the game is on the line because you might miss and be blamed for losing the game. What do you do? Do you take the shot anyway, or do you play it safe and pass the puck?"

"I take the shot."

Ice smacked me on the back so hard I stumbled forward a step. "Take the shot, rookie. Take the shot."

He winked at me and strolled off.

--Caroline--

This year the holidays were bittersweet.

I didn't have good memories of Christmas until I'd married Mark. His family celebrated in a big way, maybe too over the top, but the kids loved Christmas at their grandma and grandpa's house. The decorations were lavish and plentiful. Not even Scrooge would be able to resist getting festive once he walked into their house.

That first year, Fran had helped me decorate for the holidays. Growing up, my family's feeble attempts to decorate had ended at a scrawny fake tree with mostly broken lights and a few decorations, which would've been fine if the spirit of Christmas had resonated throughout our family. It hadn't. The holidays were an excuse for my dad to drink even more and my mother to flirt shamelessly at Christmas parties and drink her fair share.

As a new bride, I'd been overwhelmed and in awe of Mark's parents. Their house was straight out of a magazine, and I did my best to emulate Fran's holiday efforts. She taught me a lot about holiday decorating and entertaining, and I'd leaned on her talents every year. This time I was on my own, and I wasn't measuring up.

I sat at the dining room table on Christmas Eve. With great effort, I'd finally tucked my excited twins in bed. They'd fallen asleep after I read *The Night Before Christmas*.

Now to wrap their presents and fill the stockings. I'd bought each of them one extravagant present, hoping this would be a Christmas they might remember fondly despite the absence of one very important person. I was weary, mentally and physically. These past few months had been a time of upheaval and change. My first concern had been and always would be my children's well-being, which meant my needs were usually ignored, but that was what a good mother did. I never regretted one sacrifice I made for my precious, rambunctious babies.

There was a rap on my door, and I rose to answer it. Easton stood there, gripping a paper bag in one hand. My heart rate bumped up a few notches at the sight of him in all his masculine glory. No one rocked a pair of faded blue jeans like this man. He was even too sexy for words in a mere hoodie.

"Hey, you're here all alone on Christmas Eve?"

"Where else did you expect a single mother to be?"

He shrugged. "Don't know. Can I come in?"

"Okay." I stood back and let him in the door.

"Where are the kids?"

"In bed with visions of sugarplums dancing in their heads."

"What the hell are sugarplums anyway?" He grinned at me. His dark eyes sparkled with mischief, and I'd always adored his brand of mischief.

"No idea."

He pulled a bottle of eggnog out of the bag and held it up for my inspection. The bottle contained brandy, too, and I had to smile.

I snagged a couple Christmas mugs from the cupboard. He filled them with eggnog, and I sprinkled nutmeg on top. I held up my mug. "To a good Christmas."

"The best," Easton responded with one of his knock-your-socks-and-panties-off smiles. We clicked mugs and sipped the creamy liquid.

"This is yummy but surprisingly strong."

"It is." His eyes lit up like the lights on my tree. "You are joining us for Christmas dinner tomorrow, right?"

"Do I have a choice?"

"Nope." He grinned. "You don't want to miss Kaden's cooking. The guy is a genius in the kitchen. I'm salivating thinking about his prime rib."

"Why aren't you going to your cousin Cooper's house for Christmas?"

"They took a short family vacation and won't be back until the day after Christmas. So, are you going to join us?"

"I wouldn't miss it for the world." Fran had always served prime rib for Christmas dinner. It'd been absolutely to die for. I doubted Kaden would be able to top it, but I was actually looking forward to the meal. Prime rib sounded way better than the ham dinner I'd planned.

"Good." Easton stared at me intently. His scrutiny made me uncomfortable. I self-consciously wiped at my lips in fear I might have dribbled. His gaze flicked to my lips and back.

"Easton? Is something wrong?"

He almost jumped as if prodded out of his trance. "Sorry. I... You're so beautiful."

"Thank you. I don't feel beautiful."

"Well, you are."

I looked away, breaking eye contact because I didn't have the courage to hold it any longer.

Easton clutched my hand, entwining his fingers with mine, and led me to the brightly lit tree. "I missed the tree lighting."

"We knocked on your door earlier, but no one answered." His hand in mine felt so good and so right. I should've pulled away, but I didn't have the strength to resist even this simple gesture of...of what? I didn't know. Holding hands was a gesture of affection in my book, but I didn't know what was in his playbook anymore. I willed myself to stop my analysis and enjoy the moment, a hard thing for someone like me to do, but I gave it my best shot.

"I was doing some last-minute Christmas shopping."

"I see. Did you happen to buy mistletoe?" I regretted the words as soon as I'd blurted them, but what the hell, I'd own them.

He reached in the pocket of his hoodie and pulled out a sprig of mistletoe. "Never leave home without it."

"You don't? Do you wander around kissing random women all day long?"

"No, only this one." He held the mistletoe over our heads and leaned down for a soft yet toe-curling, body-melting kiss. My heart danced to the tune of the Christmas music playing in the background, as the magic of the holidays filled me with hope and joy. Yeah, I was a regular walking Christmas card. I'd tripped into a scene right out of a Hallmark Christmas movie and had no interest in changing the channel. I'd allow myself the small luxury of enjoying my fantasy a little longer.

He gazed down at me and raised his glass to clink it against mine. I'd forgotten I was holding mine and was amazed I didn't spill a drop. I sipped from the mug, never taking my eyes from him. Something in the depths of those brown eyes gave me hope, even as I warned myself not to read too much into things. He was here, and so was I.

"I'm glad you told me about the kids," he said.

"Even if it was seven years too late?"

"It's never too late. You didn't know, and as soon as you did, you contacted me. I see that now. I'm sorry for being a dick in the beginning."

"I understand. I really do. I felt so dirty, and not in a good way, finding out a man other than my husband was the father of my children, and I didn't even suspect it."

"Well, you can get dirty with me anytime. I won't mind."

There he went again, wanting us to have a sexual relationship when I was pretty sure I wouldn't be able to maintain a strictly recreational relationship with him. I stared at the tree in all its sparkling glory as confusion reigned inside me. This man had broken my heart years ago and wrecked me in the process. I wasn't sure I was strong enough to risk he'd do it again.

He set his eggnog and mine on the nearby coffee table. Standing beside me once more, he put his arm around my shoulders. I didn't pull away though I should've. Instead my traitorous body leaned into his warm, solid strength.

"How are the kids doing?"

"They're struggling without their fa—without Mark."

"It's okay. You can call him their father. He's the only father they've known." I could tell it stung him to say the words, and my ever-present state of guilt reared its ugly head, threatening to ruin the good mood I had going.

"I don't blame you anymore. We both made mistakes and handled things the best we could considering our age at the time."

"You don't?" I glanced up at him. He was smiling down at me.

"I don't. I have a confession to make, Caro."

"A confession?" My heart was beating harder than the Little Drummer Boy had on Christmas Eve all those centuries ago.

"I was too young to realize what we had wasn't easily duplicated with someone else. I thought I'd have it again when I was ready. I had the same college girlfriend for three years, and when we mutually parted ways, I was half as bothered as I was when we broke up. I had several other girlfriends, stayed with them long enough to know they weren't what I was looking for, and moved on. A couple years ago, I admitted the truth to myself. Not one of them was you, and they could never be you. I didn't know if my memory was playing tricks on me, and maybe what I recalled wasn't what was, but I had to find out. I paid for an internet background check and found your address. I drove there and sat outside your home, waiting for you. Pretty soon a guy came out of the house with one of the twins, and you came out with the other." He paused and waited for me to digest this information.

"You looked for me?"

"I did. This guy had my life, and I had hockey. I thought the tradeoff was fair, but later I wondered."

"You knew the kids were yours?"

"No, I didn't make that connection. I assumed you'd have told me if they were."

"I would've if I'd known." Was I telling the truth? If Mark had still been alive, and we'd done that DNA test, would I have told Easton? I hoped I would've.

"No more sorrys. We're beyond that, Caro. For the next two years, I tried to convince myself hockey was enough, but when I made the Sockeyes, I found myself looking around and asking myself if that was all there was, and then you came back into my life, and I was mad, mad at you for not telling me, mad at myself for cutting ties with you and causing the problem."

My heart slammed hard in my chest as I listened to his words. Unable to think of an appropriate response, I was flippant. "That must be some strong eggnog you bought," I joked, but his gaze remained serious.

"Caro. I want us to try again. Start over, as best we can. Put yesterday behind us and look ahead. I want us to be a family."

"Easton, do you know what you're saying?"

"Yeah, I do. I mean, when I walked in here, I wasn't sure what I wanted. I vacillate between just sex, friends with benefits, and something more. I didn't know what I wanted until I just verbalized my wants to you right now."

I covered my face in my hands, unable to look him in the eye, and tried to make sense of his words and make sense of my feelings. Finally, I met his gaze.

"I don't know. I don't know if we can start over. I'm not sure. We need to see how we do together, how the kids do. They don't know you're their father yet, and who knows how that'll affect them. I'm still getting over the loss of Mark. So many things are going on, and I don't want to cling to you because I'm on the rebound."

"I understand. Take all the time you need. I'll be here."

Everything about him reeked of sincerity, but I remained skeptical. Perhaps because he'd broken my heart once before after pledging his undying love and devotion for the rest of his life. Yeah, we'd been teenagers, but we weren't seasoned adults right now either. Did he mean what he said? Was he in this for the long haul through not just the good but the bad? He hadn't been tested under fire yet. The kids' meltdown earlier today had only been the tip of the iceberg.

"Would you like some help?" He gestured toward the wrapping paper, ribbon, and gifts spread across the table.

"I'd love some."

"I wrap a mean present." He winked at me.

"You'd better." I winked back.

Chapter Twenty-Two

DOG DAYS

--Easton--

*S*leeping alone wasn't how I'd wanted to spend my Christmas Eve. I'd considered more than once as I tossed and turned to text Caro and invite myself over. Only I didn't. My pride wouldn't allow me to behave in such a desperate manner, while my dick would've gladly thrown pride out the window, gotten on its knees, and begged for any crumb she might throw our way. My dick had no shame. I wasn't sure I did either.

At some point, I must've fallen asleep because the next thing I knew, it was daylight.

I wasn't a morning person, but I woke early and staggered into the kitchen for a cup of super-strong coffee. I caught a whiff of Kaden's cooking, but I was on a mission to get a cup of joe before I delved into breakfast.

Christmas morning.

My first with my kids and Caro. The first of many or the first and last?

Last night I'd been honest with her and myself thanks to Ice's hockey analogy. I'd put my heart out there and told her how I truly felt, even though I hadn't known until that very moment. I'd been so baffled by the right direction to take. To some extent, I still was, but I needed to try.

She hadn't reacted as I'd hoped, but she hadn't rejected me either. Time, we all needed time. And time we had plenty of. I was known for my patience when it came to waiting for just the right shot at the net. I'd practice that same patience with Caro. Good things came to those who waited.

I carried my cup of coffee to the living room, where Kaden and Steele sat on the couch, balancing heaping plates of bacon and eggs on their laps.

"I don't suppose you saved any for me?" I asked.

"Nope. You snooze, you lose," Kaden said.

"Asshole," I shot back.

"That's what you get for sticking us with dog-sitting duties last night while you hung with Caro."

"She was sleeping when I left," I countered.

"You're getting awful tight with her." Kaden pointed his fork at me to punctuate his words. "You're going to be paying up on that Puck Brother bet in no time. Cannot wait."

"Fuck you," I said, as it seemed to fit the occasion.

"That fucking dog ate my sock." Kaden held up a sock with a huge hole in the heel.

"At least she didn't pee on your leg like she did mine," Steele countered.

"I'm sorry, guys. I thought an older dog would be trained. I think she has a little anxiety."

"Anxiety?" Kaden snorted and rolled his eyes. "Hardly. She slept on my bed half the night and was snoring so loudly I had to sleep on the couch."

"You could've kicked her off the bed."

"Yeah, right. You try that. The dog weighs as much as I do." Kaden glared at the black Newfoundland dog sitting at his feet, staring up at him with soulful brown eyes, lines of drool stretched from her mouth to the floor.

I hadn't counted on the drooling, but I'd fallen in love with the dog's temperament. Ice and Avery had mentioned the dog last night, since she was living temporarily on the farm where his wife trained horses. I'd immediately left the party and gone to the barn to pick up Mona. She loved kids, and she was absolutely adorable, like a huge teddy bear. The twins would fall for her, but I suspected their mother would be furious.

"Mona's in love with you," Steele snickered.

"All the females love him," I quipped.

"She's in love with my cooking." Kaden glowered at the drooling dog. She took that as an invitation to jump on the couch and curl up next to him, not an easy feat considering she had to weigh one hundred and sixty pounds or more. "How much longer do we have to house this monstrous drool machine?"

"I'm giving her to Heath this morning."

"Oh, yeah, and that's going to go over well with Caro," Kaden said.

"I want to be there when you do that and watch her kick your sorry ass."

I sighed. Maybe I hadn't thought this through as well as I should've. Caro loved animals and winning her over wouldn't take long. The dog was supposed to be well trained, but I was having my doubts. She appeared to be housebroken, except for the incident with Steele, but that'd happened on the balcony, which was technically outside. I didn't know if Mona liked cats either, and that could be a deal breaker, yet I had a good idea Rusty would hold his own.

"So, guys, here's the plan. I'll go over there in about an hour, and I'll text when it's time to bring the dog over. Don't forget to wear the Santa hats." I pointed at the Sockeye Santa hats I'd bought at the team store yesterday.

My buddies rolled their eyes in unison.

"You should be grateful I wasn't able to rent any Santa and Mrs. Claus costumes this close to Christmas."

"Too bad. Kaden looks great in an apron. He could've been Mrs.

Claus." Steele winked at me. Kaden placed his plate on the coffee table and fired a pillow at him, pegging him in the head.

Steele narrowed his eyes, ready to reciprocate.

"Hey, don't throw that at me. You'll hit the dog." Mona rolled on her back, her head on Kaden's lap, and made an odd sound between a whimper and a growl. Kaden ran his hand over her long, glossy coat. "I really don't like dogs."

"She loves you."

"She's smelly and hairy and needy. Three things I avoid in a woman."

Steele threw back his head and howled. Mona's devotion to Kaden was fucking hilarious, especially considering his repulsion to animals. Mona was secretly evil and getting a kick out of torturing the one person in the house least enamored of her.

Steele and I laughed our asses off until we were exhausted. Even though the scowl on Kaden's face threatened to start us all over again, we managed to keep our emotions under control.

Kaden pushed the large dog off his lap and stood. "It's time to prep for Christmas dinner. Who's going to help?"

Steele and I exchanged glances.

"I'm delivering my presents to the kids."

"I'm taking the dog for a walk," Steele said quickly. Neither of us had any interest in peeling potatoes or chopping veggies or whatever Kaden had in mind.

"I'll take her for a spin in the park down the street and wait for your text."

"Do you have doggie bags?"

Steele reached in his pocket and withdrew a few black plastic bags. "Right here." He grabbed a leash, and Mona forgot all about the love of her life, exchanging him for a new one, the guy with the leash. She danced around until Steele corralled her long enough to put the leash on her. Together, they exited out the door.

"I sure as hell hope you know what you're doing." Kaden shook his head as he headed for the kitchen, stopped, and turned toward his room. "I'm taking a shower before I cook. I'm covered in dog slime."

I watched him go and shrugged. I didn't know what I was doing, but I was doing it anyway.

--Caroline--

The kids opened their stockings first, stuffed with chocolates and socks, a charm bracelet for Hailey, and an e-reader for Heath. They were all smiles this morning, and I breathed a sigh of relief that I hadn't seen any sadness yet, though I fully expected their loss to sink in after the thrill of Christmas morning wore off.

I insisted they eat breakfast before unwrapping the big presents. I'd spent hours fretting over what to get them and was very proud of my purchases. Both gifts had been chosen with care and consideration. I'd made lists, narrowed the options, and chosen the one perfect thing for each. They were extravagant expenditures, and I looked forward to the kids' reactions.

After breakfast, the kids ran to the tree, giddy with anticipation, while Junie sipped spiked eggnog from her perch on the couch.

Hailey bounced on the balls of her feet, while Heath clasped his hands behind his back. He, too, was excited as evidenced by his tapping foot.

"Hailey, you go first," I said, knowing Hailey would drive me crazy if she had to wait much longer.

Hailey lunged for the oddly shaped package as tall as she was and ripped off the colorful wrapping paper to reveal a lifelike, large rocking horse with a real horsehair mane and tail and a leather saddle. She screeched in delight and ran to me, throwing her arms around me. I hugged her back, blinking the tears from my eyes.

"Mommy, it's exactly what I wanted. Thank you. Thank you. Thank you. He's perfect. I'm going to call him Midnight."

Heath watched all the drama with wide eyes.

"You're next, honey."

He nodded solemnly and knelt down before his present. He carefully unwrapped it, taking care not to tear the paper. I blinked back the tears in my eyes. Sometimes Heath was his mother's son. I attacked presents in the same methodical manner. Once the paper was off, he stared at the cardboard box for a very long time without saying a thing. The contents were clearly displayed in images on the outside.

"Do you like it?" I held my breath, fearing I'd made a huge mistake.

"Yes. Thank you." He was reserved as usual, but he tore into the box with more gusto than his words showed. His gift was a puppy that walked and barked and responded to commands. The thing even did tricks. I helped him with the batteries, then watched the two of them play with their new toys. Their boisterous laughter did my heart good. So far, they were surviving their first Christmas without Mark quite well.

Rusty crawled onto my lap. With a yawn, he curled up and purred himself to sleep. Our little family was going to be okay.

Only now did I allow myself to reflect on Easton's words from the night before. He'd come looking for me two years ago after he realized I wasn't easily replaceable. I didn't know how to take that. Did we have a shot at a relationship, even being a family? I'd experienced so many changes in the past several months, I couldn't fathom what he was proposing, not yet. I needed time, and so did my children. I cared for Easton. I might even go so far as saying I'd never stopped loving him, but did we have what it took to make this work?

There was a knock at the door. I'd been expecting Easton, certain he'd come bearing gifts for the kids. I hoped he hadn't gone completely overboard, but I doubted that'd be the case. Easton had money, and he was bent on spending it.

The kids ran to the door and waited for me to look in the peep-hole. At least I was getting through to them about something. I opened the door and stood back for Easton to enter. He carried a large wrapped box. By the messy wrapping, I was certain he'd wrapped the gift himself. A lump formed in my throat over his efforts.

"Easton! Did you get me something?" Hailey jumped up and down, her little fingers grabbing for the box. Heath hung back but his eyes were bright with curiosity while he eagerly leaned forward to study the package.

"Hang on, honey. Yes, I have something for both of you." Easton set the package on the floor. "This is for you, Hailey. Heath, yours will be here in a minute."

Hailey grabbed for the ribbon and yanked it off.

"Hailey, what do you say to Easton?"

"Thank you." She paused and gazed up at him with her big blue eyes. He smiled down at her, and his eyes were suspiciously moist.

"You're welcome."

With that out of the way, she ripped the gold and green wrapping paper off and tossed it aside. The text on the box indicated it contained athletic tape, and she frowned, glancing up at Easton.

"It's the only box I could find."

Her smile returned. Easton bent down and helped her peel the tape off the top of the box and open it. Tissue was discarded as she dug through the box and finally pulled out her prize. She held it up for all to see.

"Mommy, it's a real saddle."

I gaped at him in surprise, but he avoided my gaze.

"Ice's wife, Avery, told me that's one of the best children's saddles you can buy," Easton said.

"Am I getting a pony?" Hailey screeched with excitement, and Heath scowled and held his hands over his ears. I didn't blame him. Hailey's decibel level hurt my ears at times too.

Easton didn't respond but grinned and ran his hand over the smooth leather of the saddle.

I glared at him, ready to rip him a new one—in private. A pony? We hadn't discussed this. "You did not buy her a real pony?"

"Not exactly. She'll be taking riding lessons once a week with Avery. If she loves it, then we'll talk about a pony."

Hailey threw her arms around him. "I love you, Easton!"

She hadn't told me she loved me when she'd seen the rocking horse. Easton had upstaged me. He hadn't bothered to consult me regarding his gift ideas. I was their mother. Damn it.

Jealousy curled inside me, and I fought to hold it back. His gift was too extravagant and inappropriate for someone who was currently posing as a friend of the family. I'd thought he'd understood that he'd done enough for us this year with the tree and decorations and all the money.

"A simple card would've sufficed," I growled at him in a low voice meant only for his ears.

He glanced up at me, rose to his feet, and gifted me with one of his disarming grins, making it difficult to be mad at him. "It's my first Christmas with them."

"I know, but they see you as a friend of the family. This gift is too much."

"We'll discuss your concerns later, but you know I won't back down." He glanced at his phone and tapped out a response to a text.

Heath tugged on his shirt. "Where's mine, Easton?" His soulful brown eyes just about tore my heart apart.

"On its way, buddy."

A few seconds later, the doorbell rang, and Easton opened it with a flourish. "Meet Mona!"

A gigantic beast of a dog bounded into the room and headed straight for the kids. I watched in horror, certain she'd mow them down until there was nothing left of them but two flat spots on the carpet. She slid to a stop in front of them and licked Heath's face while her madly wagging tail cleared off the coffee table.

Steele scrambled after her, grabbing for the leash she'd wrenched out of his hands. He shot us an apologetic look. "Sorry, she got away from me."

I was in a state of shock, not believing what I was seeing. Getting a face bath, Heath laughed louder than I'd heard him laugh in months, while Hailey wrapped her arms around the dog's furry neck.

"I guess I'm yesterday's news," said Kaden, stepping forward.

"Yeah, buddy, she's a fickle female. Out with the old, in with the new."

Kaden rolled his eyes. "Story of my life."

I didn't have a clue what they were talking about, but I had bigger problems. This huge, slobbering, hairy dog was the focus of my attention and Rusty's. My cat leapt onto the back of the couch, hissing and spitting, the hair raised on his back. Seemed he and I shared a mutual opinion of this monstrous dog in our domain.

Easton was on his knees, petting the dog along with the kids. His two buddies plopped down on my couch and helped themselves to Christmas cookies, oblivious to the chaos or embracing it. Junie carried a tray of mugs full of hot chocolate from the kitchen. She winked at me as she strode by. I scowled back. She and I were going to have a talk. I had a feeling she knew all about this gift.

I nudged Easton with my foot. "Can I have a private word with you?" I spoke through gritted teeth, and his guileless grin was full of fake innocence. Like he didn't have a clue what I was pissed about.

Once we were in the privacy of my room, I counted to ten before turning to face him. I was on the verge of losing my temper, and I wouldn't ruin Christmas for my kids.

"Go ahead, let me have it." He leaned against the closed door, arms crossed over his chest, and a huge, unrepentant grin on his face. His smugness infuriated me.

"What were you thinking?"

"All kids need a dog."

"That's not a dog, that's a buffalo." I paced the floor trying to work off some of my anger. "He weighs more than me and the kids combined."

"She... And I doubt she weighs that much."

"Now you're saying I'm fat?"

"No, nothing like that." Momentary panic flashed in his eyes. He'd crossed the line and was floundering to find his way back to safe footing.

"They love Mona."

"But I *do* not. Take her back where she came from."

"Not possible." His chin jutted out stubbornly. He was digging in, and I was going to have a battle on my hands.

"Anything is possible."

"I'm not returning her. The kids need a dog."

"Says who? The guy who's been a dad for a few months?"

"Yeah, that guy." His brown eyes flashed with an anger of their own.

"We're not keeping her. We can't have a huge dog like that in this condo. Who's going to take her for walks and groom her and feed her?"

"I won't lie, that would be you—and I'll help, of course. So will the guys."

"When you're here."

"She's just what Heath needs to come out of his shell."

"You're an ass. How dare you do this without running it by me first? And about the riding lessons... Horses are dangerous. I don't want my little girl getting hurt."

He suppressed a smile, which didn't go over well right now. "You're a worrier. You can't keep them from every little thing that might hurt them. Hockey's dangerous, too."

"But he's a little boy and she's a girl—"

"That's a sexist remark," he chided me, as if trying to prod me out of my serious mood and back into something lighter.

"You upstaged me. I spent a lot of time and money on their gifts, and you come in here and do this. Did you ever think about discussing your intentions with me?"

"So that's what this is about? You're jealous?" His knowing smirk raised my ire even more.

"I am not."

"Yeah, you are."

"The dog goes." I glared at him, and all he did was snort.

"Fine, you tell them."

"I will." We weren't keeping her. I pushed him away from the door and marched into the living room, ready to put an end to this dog before the kids got too attached. I stopped and stared. The dog was chasing them around the living room. The twins screamed with joy, and the dog barked joyously as drool flew everywhere.

For such a huge dog, she was amazingly gentle. She was careful not to knock the kids down, though I couldn't say the same for any furniture or accessories that lay in her path. Once they exhausted themselves, she jumped on the couch and lay down. Rusty glared at her from his perch, but she was oblivious to him. Heath crawled onto the couch beside her, wrapped his arms around her, and laid his head on her shoulder.

"I love her, Mommy. Thank you, Easton. Thank you, Mom, for letting us have a dog." Heath's brown eyes shone with such unfettered joy my heart squeezed. I never expected to see him this happy this soon, and I grudgingly had Easton to credit for his turnaround.

He'd gotten through to my son in ways his mother hadn't been able to. Yeah, I was jealous, but I was also grateful. Heath had bonded with this man who happened to be his biological father. I'd watched it happen from day one, and that bond grew every day. His daughter already adored him.

And where did that leave me in all this?

Chapter Twenty-Three

FLAMES IN THE FIREPLACE

--Easton--

I was a shithead, but I had no regrets. I'd pissed off Caro, but I'd done the right thing, even if I'd gone about it in the wrong way. Mona fit into the family as if she'd always been there. She transferred her affection from Kaden to the kids in a split second. I actually think Kaden was a little hurt by her fickleness.

Caro didn't have the heart to get rid of the dog, not as quickly as Heath attached himself to her.

"They were used for nanny dogs and water rescue. She'll be a good protector and companion," I said, parroting what Avery had told me. My cousin Riley, who was also Avery's nephew, happened to have a Newfie. I'd been impressed with the dog's calm demeanor and gentle nature. The hair and drooling were minor setbacks, the way I saw it.

The kids and I took Mona for a walk, while Caro and Junie baked some pies and Kaden worked on his Christmas dinner. When we got back, Heath and Hailey helped me set the dinner table with the

Christmas placemats and napkins I'd bought earlier this week, along with the sleigh centerpiece.

Dinner was everything I'd expected, knowing Kaden's culinary abilities. A few teammates who didn't have families in the area joined us. We ate like kings and queens. My mom was a great cook, but this holiday meal had to be one of my all-time favorites for lots of reasons.

After we finished, I proposed a toast. Everyone held up their glasses of wine or water or milk, whatever they were drinking.

"To the best Christmas ever with family and friends. May the magic of the holidays stay with us year-round." I sounded sappy, but I'd had a few and was getting sentimental.

"Hear, hear!" said the group at the table as we clinked our glasses together.

After dinner, Steele surprised us by producing a guitar and playing Christmas music. He knew all the words and was damn good. We sang along, drank too much eggnog, and ate more. Everyone pitched in, and we cleaned up. By ten p.m., the crowd dispersed with full stomachs and good memories. Junie also disappeared.

Caro wanted to go back to her condo with the kids, and I followed her, uninvited, but she didn't slam the door in my face. I considered that a good sign.

I sat down next to Caro and put my arm around her shoulders. She tensed for a moment, then leaned into me, her head on my shoulder. Having her here was the most natural thing ever. She fit next to me, and contentment washed over me.

The flame in the gas fireplace danced merrily on the opposite side of the room. The kids curled up on the thick rug with Mona, and all three of them fell asleep.

"This scene would look good on next year's Christmas card."

Caro nodded, not looking at me but staring into the flames. I wondered what she was thinking.

"Forgive me?" I whispered, leaning close to her ear.

"It's hard to stay mad at you."

"I know because I'm damn cute."

"You're a damn pain in the ass."

"That, too. The kids had a good Christmas. I wasn't sure how it'd go."

"Neither was I. They stayed busy today. Tomorrow they might crash, recalling all the past Christmases with Mark. They will feel his loss."

"It's all part of life, honey. I've been there. Losing a father is tough, but we'll be here to help them." I cupped her chin in my palm and turned her to face me. "I want many more memories like this one."

"Easton..."

"I know. I'm moving too fast."

"Like, race-car speed."

"You know me. When I decide what I want, I go after it. Caro, give us a chance."

"I want to." The hint of sadness in her voice rammed a dagger deep in my heart. She didn't believe in us. She was protecting herself and her heart from possible heartbreak. For this to work, we had to both be all in. We couldn't afford to hold back.

"I want to tell the kids I'm their father in the next few weeks."

"It's too early. Give them more time."

I sighed, weary of having the same argument with her over and over. "The more time we take, the bigger the chance someone else lets it slip. Just about everyone knows but them."

"Please, give me more time."

I was impatient for them to know so we'd be able to forge a deeper bond and they'd realize I was here to stay, but I'd respect Caro's opinions on this subject. I kissed her softly, lingering for a blissful moment.

"Let me stay the night."

She gazed up at me, her eyes searching mine. I didn't know what she was looking for, but I hoped she'd found it. She shook her head. "Not tonight." Abruptly, she stood and pointed toward the door. "I'm really tired. You probably should go. I have to get the kids to bed."

"I'll help you." Without waiting for her answer, I picked up Heath, the heavier of the twins. He didn't wake but snuggled against my shoulder, and my heart swelled with love for my boy. Caro picked up Hailey. We carried them to their respective beds. I tucked Heath in, and Mona lay down at the foot of his bed. I found Caro sitting on the edge of Hailey's bed, gazing at her daughter.

"She's beautiful, isn't she?" I put my hands on Caro's shoulders and squeezed. She looked up at me, and I saw the love in her eyes, not for me but for her children.

"They're my miracle," she said.

You're mine.

I didn't say the words, but I wanted to. The reality of those words, those deep feelings, slammed into me. If I hadn't been holding on to her shoulders, I think my knees would've buckled from the weight of my revelation.

--Caroline--

After I put the kids to bed, Easton followed me out to the living room. He didn't show any inclination toward going home. Mona followed us out of the kids' bedrooms. She had this innate sense I was the one she had to win over. She sat next to me and laid her huge head in my lap, gazing up at me with sad eyes. I was a softie for animals, and she was melting my resistance. I ran a hand over her soft fur.

Easton grinned as he handed me a glass of wine and once more took a seat next to me. The room was bathed in a glow of flickering Christmas lights from the tree. I was well-fed, content, and mellow. A peace I hadn't felt in years settled over me. I hadn't realized how much stress I'd been under when I'd been married to Mark, always trying to measure up to Mark's and his parents' standards and always falling short. I'd never been good enough. But right now at this special moment, I was good enough.

Mona nudged my hand with her wet nose, encouraging me to pet her. Easton smiled knowingly.

"She really likes you," he said.

"She likes everyone."

"Maybe. Mona had a tragic past. Ice's wife works with the Newfie rescue. She'd been in a loving family, and the father shot them all, then shot himself. She ended up in a few different homes, and they didn't take care of her. Then the rescue got ahold of her. Avery thought she'd be perfect for the kids."

"Remind me to thank Avery," I said sarcastically, but we were keeping the dog. She'd wormed her way into Heath's heart, and I wouldn't separate them. Besides, her tragic story spoke to me. "Did she witness the shootings?"

"Yeah, they found her lying in a pool of blood with her big body curled around the little boy, as if she were trying to warm him up."

"Oh, poor girl." She gave my hand a single lick as if she knew we were talking about her.

"Looks like she's won you over."

"Maybe." I wasn't giving him the satisfaction by admitting I was completely smitten with the dog. He'd suffer first for not discussing his gift ideas with me.

"I know I should've talked to you first." Easton guessed what I was thinking, but then he'd always had this weird ability to read what was in my head and my heart. "But you would've said no, and I wanted poor Mona to have a chance at a forever home with us."

With us?

I glanced up at him, and he smiled guilelessly. I'd heard him wrong. There was no *us*. Not now. Maybe not ever. I really didn't know what I wanted. It was all so confusing.

"Where's Junie?" I asked, realizing I hadn't seen her in a while.

"She went home with Steele and Kaden. They were going to play video games."

"She likes Kaden."

"Yeah, well, good luck to her. He has a mystery lover. No one's ever seen her, and he won't talk about her. Kaden is obsessed with this woman. I've never seen him like this." Easton slid his arm across the back of the couch behind me. His fingers lightly played with a lock of my hair. I involuntarily shivered from the intimate contact.

"Really? Kaden? He seems like such a player."

"He is. It's odd. Steele thinks she's married."

"Oh, that's not good for anyone."

"Tell me about it." He pulled me closer to him, and I relished the warmth of his body next to me. The gas fireplace and Christmas lights added to the magic of the moment, and I never wanted this night to end. As I stared into his deep brown eyes, I knew this was where I belonged, where I'd always belonged. I envisioned sitting in front of a Christmas tree like this with him years from now as our grandkids and great-grandkids opened their presents.

I'd thought I'd have the same future with Mark, but had I been deluding myself, or was I deluding myself now? Was the magic of the moment overriding my common sense? Falling for Easton again hadn't been part of my plan. Getting an education and supporting my children comfortably without anyone else's help had been. I started classes after the new year, working toward my nursing degree. It'd be difficult to study and take care of rambunctious twins, but I would find a way. I had Junie's help, and I had Easton's. He was a great father, even if he didn't have much practice. The kids adored him, and I'd abandoned my fears he wasn't in this for the long haul.

"What are you thinking?" he said as he smiled at me.

"About us." My honesty surprised him. I saw it in his eyes. His expression softened, and he pulled me closer to him. I didn't resist. I wasn't capable of resistance. I'd been resisting him for too long, and tonight I didn't have the willpower or the energy. I rested my head on his strong, capable shoulder and cleared my overactive brain of as many worries as possible, allowing myself to just be for a little while.

We sat there in silence, listening to Christmas music and watching the flames dance in the fireplace.

Chapter Twenty-Four

A BIG STEP

--Caroline--

woke much later. At first, I was disoriented, but my foggy brain finally registered where I was. Easton was carrying me to the bedroom. He nudged the door shut with his heel and placed me on the bed. I lay there, looking up at him, as I fully awoke. I'd had dreams, dreams of Easton and me together. In one dream, Mark pounded on the door of our happy home and demanded I come back to him. He wasn't really dead, and I was still married to him. That one shook me up more than I cared to admit.

Easton sat on the edge of the bed. "What's wrong, Caro? I saw something in your eyes. What is it?"

"Just a disturbing dream."

"Tell me about it. You can tell me anything."

Déjà vu washed over me. He'd said those words to me years ago, and I'd spilled the truth about my horrible homelife and unloving parents. I'd been certain then I hadn't been worthy of love, that something had to be wrong with me, not them. Even now, I still suffered from the residual effects of feeling unloved and unworthy. Trust had always been an issue with me. Loving Mark had been safe because our love wasn't the soul-deep kind of love that would rip your heart out and leave you irreparably scarred and broken if it ever ended.

"Caro, I'm here for you. I won't walk away again. I promise."

"I'm trying." I wanted to believe him, but my life had been about the people I loved the most leaving me. Getting beyond that kind of programming wouldn't be easy.

He lay down next to me, fully clothed, and held me in his arms. He didn't try anything, just held me. "You don't have to be strong all the time. I have broad shoulders. I can carry some of the load too."

His words rang true, but I wasn't that easy to win over. I held back a part of me, a part I'd once given to him and only him. He'd stomped the life out of me and left me alone and, unknown to us, pregnant. Trust would take time.

"So can I stay?" He rolled onto his side and propped his head on his hand.

I wanted him to stay, but I was compelled to resist out of pure habit. "The kids might hear us."

"These walls are pretty soundproof," he assured me. "And the doors are solid wood."

"And you know this how?"

He gave me one of *those* looks. "Seriously? You're asking me this? Look who I'm rooming with."

"Steele, who keeps to himself and doesn't bring women home, and Kaden, who has a secret lover no one knows anything about."

"You do have a point. As long as you tamp down your screaming, we should be fine."

"My screaming?"

"I used to make you scream. In fact, I loved it when you screamed out my name."

I'd loved it, too, but I wasn't telling him what he already knew. "I don't scream anymore."

"Let me see what I can do about that."

"I'm mad at you."

"Makeup sex is the best."

"Do you have an answer for every argument I come up with?"

"Yup." He grinned at me. One of his large hands stroked my arm. His eyes shone with affection and desire. "I haven't slept with anyone since you called me that first time."

"No one?"

"No one measures up to you."

I'd had the same problem, but out of respect to Mark, I didn't voice my opinions. "Kiss me."

He did, starting soft and careful and growing to roughly demanding with a good dose of need. Rolling me onto my back, he continued his sweet assault on my mouth. I slid my hands under his shirt and reveled in the warm skin under my fingertips. The muscles in his back flexed as his hands and mouth moved down my body, exploring and touching. He started with my jaw and neck and my collarbone. Soon, my sweater was pushed upward and over my head. I leaned forward and lifted my arms to help him. He pulled off his shirt and tossed both of them aside.

"Easton," I groaned as his mouth settled on the swell of my breast. He unhooked the back of my bra with none of the fumbling of the teenage Easton. This Easton was a man with much more experience, and he was familiar yet different.

He slid his tongue around my nipple, sucking it into his mouth, as I moaned and writhed underneath him. He thumbed my other nipple, pressing and pinching gently. His touch sent shockwaves through my body. I hadn't realized how much I'd missed this. Missed him.

Then he was gone. The absence of his weight left me cold and shivering, a void only he could fill.

"I'm sorry. I'm not going to be able to do much in the way of foreplay this time. I have to have you." He kicked off his shoes and yanked off his pants and underwear. I smiled as I saw his erection, knowing it was all for me. He peeled the remainder of my clothes off me and fished a condom from his pocket.

"You came prepared?" I arched my back, not the least bit modest regarding my current nakedness. He'd seen me before, and he'd see me again. No doubt about that. I spread my legs, waiting for him, as I opened my mouth and ran my tongue around my lips while staring pointedly at his cock.

His grinned down at me. "You'll get your chance, but I have to fuck you first. I don't think I would be able to hold out for much else tonight."

"We can take it slow later." I reached for him, and he came to me. His handsome face flooded with emotions I didn't dare to interpret. Right now, right here, he was mine, and I was his. Tomorrow was tomorrow, and for now it didn't matter. We mattered. We'd always mattered, even through those years we'd been apart.

He entered me, and my body gladly stretched to accommodate him. We were where we belonged. He moved inside me, and I buried my fingers into his back, urging him to go deeper until he touched me so deep I felt as if he'd found that piece of my soul I'd kept hidden from the world.

This wasn't just sex. It wasn't just fucking. It was something beautiful yet carnal, profound yet part of the cycle of life. We bonded. Our bodies melded together. Our souls entwined.

We came together in a powerful surge of emotions that rolled over me with the intensity of a rocket launch. My mind left my body and merged with his. He loved me. I felt it. I knew it. I wanted it.

And I loved him.

Tomorrow I might regret what I'd done, but tonight, no regrets.

--Easton--

Someone shook me awake. I didn't want to wake up. I was having an erotic dream in which Caro and I were on a warm beach. As I moved inside her, warm waves rolled over us again and again.

"Easton, wake up."

I groaned and rolled onto my stomach, burying my head in the pillow. The dream was too good to leave it behind just yet.

"Easton! Wake up!" Caro's voice was urgent.

Alarmed, I rolled to my back and sat up. "Is something wrong?" I rubbed my eyes and tried to get my bearings. I wasn't one of those guys who woke up and hit the ground running. It took several minutes and a few cups of coffee before I was semi-functional.

"It's six a.m. You have to get out of here before the kids and Junie know you stayed the night."

"Why?" I sat up in bed and squinted at the early-morning light peeking through the slats in the blinds. All I wanted to do was crawl back under the covers with Caro and spend the morning making love to her. When had fucking become making love? I mused.

She gave me one of those *how can you be so dense* glares. I blinked several times. She was in a bathrobe, standing at the foot of the bed, staring at me. I heard a scratch at the door. Mona needed to go out.

"Take the dog for a walk, would you? I need to clean up and get breakfast ready."

I staggered to my feet and began gathering my clothes, pulling them on. "What time is breakfast?"

She frowned, and I half expected her to tell me I wasn't invited. "In an hour."

"Great. I'll be back." I gave her a kiss on the cheek, ignoring the cool reception. She was having morning-after regrets, and I understood her feelings. I'd let things go for now. One step at a time. And last night had been a big step.

Chapter Twenty-Five

SPACE NEEDED

--Caroline--

W hat had I done?

I'd given in to my lust without giving a fuck about the long-term consequences. Yeah, sleeping with Easton had been epic, like a dream come true. Now it was morning, and my dream turned to harsh reality.

I was a fool and an idiot, and I was now deeper into this mess than I'd ever been. I was scared and fearing I'd never measure up to all those other women chasing after Easton. My insecurities ran rampant this morning, and I regretted last night, even while I had to admit I'd do it again given the opportunity.

The kids woke up shortly after Easton left to walk the dog. We'd almost gotten caught.

My phone rang, displaying Fran's name. Oh, my God, I'd forgotten to return their call yesterday. Now I really felt like shit. In all the chaos that was Christmas and my mixed-up feelings regarding Easton, I'd completely left out two of the best people in my life on the biggest family holiday of the year.

"Fran, I'm so sorry we didn't call you back yesterday."

I moved out of the living room and down the hall to my bedroom. Bad idea. The bedroom reminded me of last night and Easton. I hurried back to the hallway.

"That's not like you, Caro. It was Christmas day, for God's sake, and we didn't get to talk to our only grandchildren. I know they're not blood, but they're our grandkids. Have you already forgotten us?" Fran was understandably upset, and I deserved her anger.

"I'm so sorry." As busy as I was, the Mills were important to my children and to me.

"How quickly you've moved on, Caro. It's as if none of us ever existed. Did you take even a moment to remember Mark yesterday? Did all those wonderful Christmases we spent together as a family mean nothing to you? We loved you like the daughter we never had. We treated you well, and this is the thanks we get?"

I'd never heard Fran so upset. Guilt crushed me with the force of an elephant sitting on my chest. I was a horrible person. Really horrible.

"Fran, I know words can't fix this, but I'm truly sorry."

"I'm hurt, really hurt, Caro. Sorry isn't going to fix this. I'd rather not talk to you. Please put the grandkids on the line."

"Here's Hailey." I handed the phone to Hailey. "It's your grand-mother, sweetie."

Hailey grabbed the phone and took it into her bedroom, jabbering excitedly. Heath hurried after her, patiently waiting for his turn. I trudged to the kitchen, bearing the huge weight of guilt. I'd messed up. I'd been so wrapped up in the holidays and Easton, I'd forgotten about Fran and Howard.

I heard a rap on the door and opened it for Easton and Mona to enter.

He took one look and my face and said, "What's wrong?"

"I forgot to have the kids call their grandparents yesterday." I was miserable. I'd brought this on myself, and I had no one else to blame. My attention had been focused solely on myself, Easton, and the kids.

No one else had entered my tight little world yesterday. I'd barely thought of Mark. This had been my first Christmas without him, and I'd forgotten the man I'd spent seven years with as if he'd never existed. He'd been there for me when Easton hadn't. He'd loved my children and given me a good life. His parents had loved me as their own. They'd supported me and always been there for me, and this was how I repaid them. I was an awful person, and I'd betrayed them. I'd betrayed Mark. I'd betrayed my children.

"Oh." Easton watched me warily, as he skirted around me to the coffeepot and poured a cup for him and me. He turned back, handing me a cup. "Was it ugly?"

"Beyond ugly. I'm horrible. How quickly I forgot about them and about Mark. The guy I spent the last several Christmases with. Fran is hurt, and she has every right to be. The kids are talking to them now." I sipped the strong coffee and avoided his gaze.

Easton's troubled gaze flicked to the hallway, where the bedrooms were.

"I betrayed them all. I dismissed all my memories of them as if they never existed. What kind of person does that?"

"One who's healing?" Easton offered lamely, uncomfortable with this subject.

"Or undeserving of such good people in her life?"

"No, Caro, you're not like that. You deserve happiness, too. You forgot. There was so much going on. It's understandable."

"No. It is not. What I did is unforgivable."

"I wouldn't go that far—"

"You should leave." The deadness in my tone surprised me, and the hurt in Easton's eyes didn't help my mood any. I'd been a selfish bitch yesterday and partially because of my infatuation with him.

"I want to stay." Easton lifted his chin stubbornly. He wasn't going anywhere. There was nothing that would defuse the bomb about to go off once the fuse was lit.

"You don't belong here. You need to leave."

My words were blunt and even cruel. I'd take them back if I could, but it was too late.

--Easton--

I don't belong here?

I froze, unable to move as Caro's words sliced deep, like a dagger to the heart. She didn't waver. The coldness on her face didn't thaw. She was upset and taking it out on me. I was the easiest target because of her guilt over what we did last night.

Understanding her behavior didn't make me feel any better.

"They're *my* children too." If she wanted cold, I could do cold. My words dripped ice, and my face froze into an emotionless mask.

We stared each other down, both poised for battle, even if we weren't sure what we were battling over. If this was how parenthood with her would be, we had a long way to go. With my parents, it had been a collaborative process, not a combative one. Caro hadn't had the good examples I'd had from her own dysfunctional family.

"Not yet, they aren't. They don't know who you are. I'm sure they have questions, but as you can see, now is not the right time to introduce a new man into their lives. I knew better, and I let my own selfish desires get in the way of what's best for my children."

What was she saying? Was she telling me to butt out of her life and my kids' lives? I wouldn't do that. Not now that I'd gotten a taste of fatherhood. I didn't care how uncomfortable my presence made her. My kids needed me, and I needed them. I wasn't backing off. I wasn't going away. They were my flesh and blood.

"You want me to make this easy on you and disappear?"

She narrowed her eyes and glared at me.

Before we had a chance to say another word to each other, Hailey marched out of the bedroom with Heath at her side. One look at their faces and I suppressed a cringe. They were furious. Mona, sensing the tension in the air, quickly went to Heath's side. He wrapped one arm around her neck but didn't bat an eyelash.

"Why didn't you have us call Grandma yesterday? She's sad. We miss her and Grandpa. We miss our daddy." Hailey threw back her head and wailed. Tears streamed down her face. Accusation and the agony of loss dulled her blue eyes. Her sobs were heartbreaking, and I was at a total loss, but I had to do something.

"Hailey, honey, your mommy didn't mean—"

"You're not my daddy," she screamed at me, and her words punched me harder than a puck to the gut.

She stomped down the hallway to her bedroom. Heath glared angrily at both of us before racing after her, Mona loping behind him. A few seconds later, the door slammed.

Caro turned on me. "I told you to leave. Please go, and let me take care of this mess."

I was completely out of my comfort zone. I didn't know what to do, so I did what she asked. I paused with my hand on the door. "I leave tomorrow for a road trip."

"Fine. Contact me when you return."

I'd been given the boot out the door and told quite clearly not to come back in the near future. With my tail tucked between my legs, I slinked out the door and back to my own condo.

I was shaking by the time I entered the condo. Steele was home, and he glanced up as I entered. "You look like hell. That's not what I expected after you spent the night at Caro's."

"We had a fight this morning." The most incredible night of my life had been ruined by one of the most upsetting mornings I'd ever had.

"What kind of fight?"

"Over the kids. She wants me to back off."

"You are getting pretty tight with them."

"They're my fucking kids," I almost shouted, and Steele's brows shot upward as he studied me.

"You don't have to rush this. You're pushing too hard. Back off. They're all dealing with a tragic death. Give them time."

"Spoken like someone who knows."

"Yeah, I know. It hurts. You lost your own dad. How would you feel if a new guy tried to take his place within a few months of his death?"

"Pissed."

"Yeah, well, cut them some slack and give them some space. You've been hovering ever since they moved in. This road trip will be good for you."

He was right. I'd give them space. I didn't have much of a choice considering we'd be gone on a road trip for a few days, returning on New Year's Eve. I'd been so looking forward to the new year. Now things weren't looking quite as bright.

I'd been pushing. I'd back off and give everyone some space to grieve.

Chapter Twenty-Six

CONTROL

--Easton--

*H*ockey, I needed to concentrate my energy on hockey.

The Sockeyes had won the Cup last season, and all eyes were on us this season. We were also rebuilding, having lost key players to free agency and retirement. We were still in the hunt with over half the season to go. The defending champs would make the playoffs, but doing a repeat on the Cup was next to impossible.

Regardless, our captains wanted to win it all again, and so did the rest of us. As rookies, Kaden, Steele, and I all had lifelong dreams of one day hoisting the Cup high over our heads and skating around the arena with it while the crowd cheered.

My team was battling for the second spot in the division. We won the first away game of the road trip. Tomorrow we'd fly to Vegas.

Despite the upheaval in my life, I was playing well, one of the top rookies of the year. Coach Coop was pleased with my performance as was the head coach. I'd had a good game tonight, and I was proud of myself. My troubles with Caro and the kids hadn't affected my play. I guess that meant I was growing up and turning into a true professional.

I walked into the hotel lounge after our away game, whistling a tune I'd probably picked up from one of the kids' television shows. I'd planned on going straight to my room, but I was too wired to sleep, so I was left with nothing to do but seek out my cohorts. I was missing Caro and the kids way more than I cared to admit. I'd fallen for her again. The sex had been better than ever, and I adored her company.

Several heads turned toward me. The Puck Brothers sat at a table, their expressions grim.

"Easton, come over here." Ziggy motioned me over.

I grabbed a beer from the bar and ambled over. Cautiously, I studied each one of them. Something was up. I pulled a chair from the table and sat down in it, grinning at them.

"Somebody die?" I asked.

They continued to stare at me, not one change of expression. This group was all about a good time, and they were being way too serious for my taste.

With Axel still in the minors, Ziggy appeared to be the spokesman of the group. He cleared his throat, not seeming to want to broach the subject, but he finally spit out the words he'd been holding back. "You're not behaving like a Puck Brother."

"I guess that depends on how you define Puck Brother. I'm not married. I'm not living with a woman. I'm just spending time with my kids, and she happens to be their mother." What I'd been doing was way more than that, but my feelings for Caro were private and sacred, and I didn't want to reveal my innermost thoughts to these clowns. They'd use anything they perceived as a weakness for fodder to harass me or play jokes on me. I didn't care to be the brunt of their jokes.

"You're hot for her," Kaden said.

"Yeah, so? You're hot for the mystery woman."

Kaden scowled, but that shut him up. Steele said nothing. He didn't throw me under the bus like he could've, mentioning I'd been kicked out of Caro's condo.

"I'm still a brother. I'll always be a brother, even if I'm no longer single. We're all buddies, right?"

"Yeah, right," they mumbled and nodded as one. We held up our beer bottles in a toast to each other.

"Besides," I added. "We've decided to cool it for a while so she can concentrate on her education and I can concentrate on my game."

All eyes studied me skeptically. They didn't buy what I was selling. I shrugged. They could take it as the truth or leave it. Didn't matter to me.

"Is being in love grounds for being kicked out of the Puck Brothers?" Kaden mused.

"We didn't discuss that point," Steele said with total seriousness. "I knew we need to write that shit down, like our rules and stuff."

A collective groan reverberated around the table.

"I'm not losing the bet." Not yet, anyway. "And I'll still be a Puck Brother. We're all brothers on the ice, and we play with a puck. And Kaden is just as guilty of monogamy as I am."

No one disputed my statement, and I successfully diverted their attention to Kaden.

"So, Kaden..." Cave turned the attention to my roomie, and I sat back to watch the fireworks. "Who is this mystery woman?"

Kaden's smile faded, and he closed off completely. "No one you fuckheads know."

"Why the secrecy? You bringing her to Ice's New Year's Eve party?"

"I don't know. I'll ask her. She doesn't like parties much." Something in his eyes indicated he was lying, and one of the guys jumped on it.

"How the hell did you ever meet her then?"

"At a club in Portland."

"She lives in Portland?" Ziggy asked.

"I don't know." Kaden took a long pull on his beer and avoided our astonished gazes. He didn't know where she lived? His response was mind-boggling.

"What's up with this woman? Is she in witness protection or something?" Cave asked.

"She's very private. I don't ask too many questions, and neither does she. She doesn't even know I play hockey or my real name. I probably don't know hers either. This is fun and secretive and sexy. That's all."

We exchanged glances with each other and dropped the subject.

--Caroline--

The next few days were tense, but finally the kids worked their way out of their funk, and I was no longer public enemy number one.

"When is Easton coming back?" Heath asked me at the dinner table, as he shoveled in enough spaghetti to feed two teenage boys, or so it seemed to me. Mona lay under the dining table at Heath's feet. She'd figured out pretty fast the kids spilled stuff and slipped her goodies during their meal.

Heath's question surprised me. Neither of my children had mentioned Easton since the phone call with Fran. I'd broken Fran's heart with my selfish actions, and I hated myself for it. She'd never been anything but good to me. This holiday had to be hard on them after the death of their son, and I'd spent the day without giving them or their son a thought, while fucking Easton that night.

I'd tried to call Fran and Howard a few times since, but my calls went unanswered. My kids loved the Mills and so did I. They were the only grandparents they had. My own parents had been nonexistent in their lives. They needed as many stabilizing factors as possible. And Fran and Howard were stable examples. They were good people, and I knew they'd get over their hurt and come around. I even bought a card, wrote a heartfelt note, and mailed it to them.

We finished our meal, and the kids curled up on the couch with Rusty and Mona to watch a movie. Junie helped me wash dishes and clean the kitchen.

"Have you heard from Easton?" She knew all about the issues with Fran and me kicking Easton out of the condo that morning.

"He's texted me a few times. Just asked how things were going."

"Did you respond?"

"No. I let him too far into my life. Now it's time to back him out. He might be the kids' biological father, but he hasn't earned the right to be called Dad."

Junie arched a brow and shook her head.

"What?"

"He hasn't earned the right? Listen to yourself."

"I don't know what you're getting at. Spell it out."

"You want him to be part of their lives, but you want full control. Isn't parenting a combined effort?"

"Well, yeah."

"Mark let you deal with the kids. He was the fun dad who didn't discipline them. He left the hard stuff to you. Maybe Easton wants more of a partnership. Have you discussed this with him?"

"Absolutely not."

"Because you're not willing to give up full control." When Junie's voice took on that superior tone, it grated on my last nerve.

"They're my children. I have control. He does not."

"I don't think he sees it that way. You gave up full control when you contacted him. Don't you see that?"

I hung my head. I did see that, but I fought it every step of the way.

Chapter Twenty-Seven

AT AN IMPASSE

~~Easton~~

The next day was a travel day and then we'd play a game in Vegas the following night and return to Seattle after the game and in time for New Year's Eve.

Once we landed, I deposited my bags in the room and ran into Ziggy in the hotel bar. Most of our teammates had taken off to a casino across the street.

"What are you doing here?" I was surprised. Ziggy was the biggest partier on the team. He never missed a chance to party it up.

"Just taking it easy for once." Ziggy shrugged. Something was bothering him, but I wasn't one to push. If he wanted to tell me, he would. As far as I knew, he might be nursing the mother of all hangovers. A guy had to take a break once in a while.

"What about you? You're not hanging out with the bros either."

Ziggy and I had never been tight, but for some reason, I unloaded on him about the kids and Caro. He was a shockingly good listener and didn't say anything until I was done with the entire sordid story.

"So, she's pretty much kicked your ass to the curb this time?"

"Seems like it."

"Are you still in love with her?"

I frowned, opened my mouth to protest his use of *still* and *in love*, then thought better of it. I didn't know if what I felt for her as a teenager was love or lust or a combo of both, but it'd been real and intense and all-consuming in a way that only teenagers could love. This thing I felt now was more mature and scarier in its ability to deeply hurt me. Then there was the complication of the kids.

"I don't know if what I feel is love." I was being brutally honest or so I thought. "Besides, I'm a Puck Brother." I grinned at him, attempting to lighten the mood.

"Yeah, so? You need to protect your interests in those kids. You said you have some temporary papers signed?"

"Just outlining the amount of monthly support until we settled everything."

"Have you considered adopting them?"

I ran a thumb over the stubble on my chin, considering his words. "I hadn't thought that far ahead."

"You want them to have your last name, don't you? You need an undisputable claim to them as your children, don't you?"

Possessiveness swelled within me. They were my kids, damn it, even if they didn't know it. "Yeah, I do."

"And when are you going to tell them you're their father? Time's a wasting, buddy. As long as they don't know, she maintains the ultimate control. You need to get a handle on that. You've waited long enough. Waiting much longer is only going to make it worse."

"You know, Zig, you're right. I'm glad you were hanging out here tonight. I needed someone with a fresh perspective to help me see through this mess."

"I'm your man." Ziggy raised his beer glass, and we toasted, each taking a long pull before setting down our glasses.

"She's going to hate me when I approach her with all this."

"Maybe, but put the kids first, not her feelings. She's collateral damage."

I didn't like his words. He made this sound like a battle, and I didn't want a battle. I wanted us to be on the same page and supportive of each other's decisions. Maybe I was dreaming and that'd never happen.

"What's the deal with Kaden?" Ziggy swiftly changed the subject, and I was grateful for the respite. I needed more time to think this through, figure out the right approach that'd do the least amount of damage.

"No one knows. He has a secret lover. They sneak off to hotels together at the oddest times, and no one has seen them in public."

"She's married. I've had a few relationships like that. All the telltale signs are there, especially the secretive meetings and minimal information about who she is. All red flags."

"Yeah, that's what I'm thinking."

"A hookup is one thing, but he's gone way beyond a couple nights. Getting mixed up with a married woman leads to nothing but grief. I don't have too many rules when it comes to dating women, but avoiding the married ones is at the top of my list."

"Mine too," I agreed, but my mind was elsewhere. Ziggy focused his attention on one of the bar TVs showing highlights from the night's game, in which I'd scored a goal, and Ziggy had an assist. The coach put us on the second line together, along with veteran Scott Monet, and we'd been on fire. Usually it took several games for a line to gel, but we played as if we'd been together for years. Maybe we'd gotten lucky tonight and were in the zone, but I'd take it, whatever it was.

My professional life was on track, and I needed to fix my personal life once I figured out how I wanted to fix it. Did I want to pursue Caro, despite her resistance to being with me, her need to stay in control, and her stubborn refusal to listen to reason?

Yeah, I did.

I'd make her listen. Living in limbo wasn't fun for any of us.

--Caroline--

The morning of New Year's Eve, I woke to a typical gray Seattle day. I didn't have any plans to celebrate other than hang out with my kids and maybe drink a glass of cheap champagne at midnight. Junie had plans to go out with Steele and Kaden, which was fine with me. She'd been hovering, and I'd been so despondent about the kids' meltdown and my conversation with Fran.

Our doorbell rang. I looked up from the game I was playing with the kids and shot Junie a questioning glance. She shrugged and went to the door to answer it.

Easton walked into the condo, and the kids immediately leapt to their feet and ran to him. Mona bounded to his side, her entire butt wagging and drool flying. He hugged Heath and Hailey, patted Mona, then turned to me, one large hand on each child's shoulder. I was struck one more time with how comfortable they were with Easton and how right they looked together.

"Can we talk?" His tone was unreadable, not giving me a clue as to the subject of this conversation.

"Uh, sure."

"I'll leave you two to discuss. Kids, help me walk Mona." Junie glanced from one of us to the other. She helped Hailey and Heath put on their coats, grabbed a leash for Mona, and they were out the door, and we were alone.

He sat on the barstool, so I sat on the one next to him. After running his hands over his face, Easton met my gaze. "I don't know how to start this conversation. I think we should see if we can make this work."

"This? What do you mean by *this*?" I wrung my hands together, not sure what he was getting at.

"You, me, the kids. Being a family." He reached for my hand again and squeezed it. "We're in this together whether we like it or not."

"We are?" Of course we were. What a stupid question.

"Yeah, we are. We also have this insane chemistry between us. I'm tired of denying it when you creep into my thoughts no matter how hard I try to keep you out."

He crept into my thoughts, too, probably way more than he imagined. "I don't know." I wasn't willing to concede just yet. My husband hadn't been dead all that long, along with a thousand other reasons this wouldn't work.

"At least say you'll think about it."

"I'll think about it."

He nodded. "Caro, there are a few other things we need to handle."

Here it came. I should've known there was a catch. I held my breath while every muscle in my body tensed, preparing me for the worst.

"I want to adopt the kids, but first we have to tell them I'm their dad. If we don't do it soon, they may find out by accident. Too many people know. It could get out publicly. Besides, I want them to have my last name, not Mills, and I have that right. And not hyphenated. I can't do that. I wish I was a big enough man to say I could, but I can't. They're my blood."

And the hits kept on coming. Easton wanted to adopt the children so they'd have his last name? But then they wouldn't have Mark's last name or my last name.

I was losing my babies, whether I liked it or not. The more legal control Easton had over them, the less I had.

The kids were already crazy about him. Little by little, they fell deeper under his spell. I, too, struggled to resist his charms, so I didn't know how two small children would ever be able to resist, nor would they want to once they found out he was their father.

The other thing I grappled with was trust. I wasn't certain I trusted him. I'd always had trust issues because of my own parents, who'd made promise after promise and never followed through. How did I know Easton wouldn't betray me, too? What made me such a good judge of character to think Easton would have my back when it might not be to his advantage to do so?

I met his gaze with a steady one of my own. "No, I won't let you adopt them and change their last name. I owe Mark that much."

His mouth thinned into a grim line and his jawed tightened. He glared at me, and I glared back. "You're being unreasonable. I can protect them."

"From who? Me?"

His anger faded to hurt. "You think I'd do that to you?"

"I don't know what to think. I'd appreciate it if you'd leave my home." I stood, holding on to the counter until I had my bearings.

"Caro, don't do this."

"Don't do what?"

"Let's discuss this. Talk about it."

"You're not adopting them. There's nothing to discuss. They're my children."

With his face a tense mask, he stood and strode toward the front door. I followed him. With his hand on the knob, he turned and said grimly, "They're my children, too, Caro. Don't you forget that. Nothing will stand in my way of being their father. Nothing."

I believed him. I also believed I was being the stubborn one, yet I couldn't help myself. Instead of calling him back for a civil discussion, I let him go.

The room was empty and lonely the second he left. As if all the joy had been sucked out of it with his final words. He hadn't delivered a threat, he'd delivered a promise.

Chapter Twenty-Eight

WHAT I WANTED

--Easton--

*R*ight after New Year's Day, the team left on another road trip, and I was somewhat relieved to get out of town and away from my problems with Caro. The road trip gave me the time to clear my head and study the situation with a logical eye.

Caro thought I was the enemy, and I was far from the enemy. We both wanted what was best for Hailey and Heath. Couldn't she see we shouldn't be at odds?

I'd gone over and over our argument in my head until I was driving myself crazy. The only time I was able to banish her from my mind was on the ice. Our first away game of the road trip was with New Jersey. We played a hard-fought game but lost by one goal. Afterward the locker room was quiet. We hadn't played well, and we were mad at ourselves. I'd played like crap, one of my worst games so far as an NHL player. Kaden and Steele hadn't played any better. In fact, the entire team had been sluggish and uninspired.

Coach Gorst entered the room, flanked by his assistants. They were all grim-faced. We hung our heads low and waited for the dressing-down to come, and come it did. Gorst laid into us, berated us for sloppy puck handling, careless passes, shots so far off the net we appeared to be shooting for the glass. We deserved it, all of it.

None of us said a word as Gorst paced the floor and ranted. Not one guy was immune to his anger. He rattled off examples of crappy play by each one of us, not even stopping once to consult his clipboard. He'd committed our transgressions to memory. He stopped to take a breath during his tirade, and you could hear a pin drop in the locker room, except for—

I took a chance and glanced around the room as did several others.

What the fuck was that noise?

"Frontier! Are you snoring?" Coach whipped around and jabbed a finger at the offending player. A few of my teammates snickered and earned a scathing glare from the coach, which shut them up fast.

All heads turned to our backup goalie, Jacques "Jock" Frontier. He was a seasoned veteran who never caused problems, a real team player, always helping us young guys. Jock jerked to attention.

"Uh, sorry, Coach." The man's face flushed with embarrassment. I can say in all honesty, every one of us was grateful Gorst's wrath wasn't focused on us.

"Sorry? You're sorry? What the fuck does that mean? You're sorry you're not fully engaged with this team enough to listen to what I have to say? You've disrespected me, your coaches, your teammates, and yourself."

Poor Jock slouched lower on the bench and studied his feet. His face was flushed bright red. I felt sorry for him, but I kept my sympathy to myself. Nobody crossed Gorst when he was in one of his moods.

Gorst barked out a few more words, then stomped from the locker room with his assistants in tow.

Next to me, Jock rubbed his eyes. I noticed he had big bags under them. He was one of those quiet guys who was often forgotten. He went about his job and never asked for attention or praise. "Not sleeping?" I asked.

"I have five little kids. What do you think?"

"I think sleep would be a luxury."

He nodded. "I look forward to road trips."

"I can understand that."

I didn't know much about Jock. He was in his late thirties, and he rarely attended team events. His wife didn't come to any of his games or hang out with the other WAGs, but with five kids, no one questioned her absence. I certainly didn't.

"Don't get me wrong. I love my kids, but it's hard with that many."

"I'm sorry he nailed you like that."

"I deserved it." Jock shrugged. "I hear you're a new father. How's that going?" Typical Jock, he took the focus off him and put it on others.

"It's going well with the kids, but they don't know I'm their father yet."

"Oh, that's rough. When are you planning on telling them?"

"As soon as their mother approves it." I sounded more irritated than I meant to. Jock arched a brow at me but didn't say much.

"You'll find fatherhood is the most rewarding and most challenging thing you've ever done. Playing in the NHL is far easier."

"I believe you."

"Enjoy every beautiful, frustrating moment. They grow up too fast."

"I will. I've missed enough as it is." Once again, bitterness crept into my voice.

"You might want to get over that attitude before it affects your children. Forgive and move on. They're here now, and that's what matters."

"I'm trying."

"Try harder." Jock gave me a sad smile and moved to his locker to get out of his gear. I watched him go and wondered how a man with a loving family could be so sad.

--Caroline--

The new year was almost three weeks old.

Nothing was resolved between Easton and me. In fact, he avoided being alone with me as I did him. While we hadn't discussed it, we appeared to be taking a break from each other, and I couldn't say if this break was temporary or permanent. I was dealing with a lot of emotional shit, trying to get my head on straight, and I'd started classes at a nearby college.

I'd backed off and allowed Easton to take the kids without requiring my presence. It was easier on both of us this way. I also gave the school permission for Easton to pick them up after school on occasion. If Hailey and Heath thought it was weird they spent so much time with a friend of the family, they never voiced their concerns.

Guilt hung over my head like the gray clouds dominating the Seattle skies, and I labored to find the sunshine. Guilt over deceiving my children about Easton. Guilt over betraying my dead husband. Guilt over forgetting Fran and Howard over Christmas. And most of all, heart-wrenching guilt at my weak-willed heart to fall once again for a certain sexy hockey player.

Today, that hockey player had picked them up for the team's family skate, something the Sockeyes did a few times a year at the practice facility. He'd invited me, but I'd politely declined, even though part of me really wanted to go. I loved to skate and skating with Easton and my kids would be like a dream come true.

After they left, I paced the floor until I'd just about driven myself batshit crazy. I fretted about everything, and right now I happened to have a lot to fret about. Stopping in mid-pace, I drew in a breath and let it out slowly. I needed to do something productive.

My eyes were drawn to my cell resting several feet away on the coffee table. I had the ability to relieve myself of one worry, and I needed to do this one thing.

With determination, I marched to the phone, picked it up, and called Fran. I'd tried to contact her a few times since Christmas with no luck. Hopefully, I'd get through today.

The phone rang six times before I heard a hesitant "Hello."

"Fran?" I swallowed hard and cleared my throat, hoping I didn't sound like the basket case I was becoming.

"Caro." Fran's tone was neutral, and I'd take that as a good sign.

"I've been trying to reach you."

"I know, honey."

Her calling me honey had to be a good thing, and I jumped on it. "I'm so sorry. I miss you and Howard." My last few words came out as a strangled sob.

The silence stretched through time and space. I glanced at my display to assure myself she hadn't hung up. She was still connected.

"Fran?" I said in a shaky voice.

"I'm sorry too. I had to take a little time to sort out my feelings. The funny thing is I was going to call you this morning."

Finally, she'd spoken, and I flopped onto the couch because my knees refused to hold me upright. "I can't express how sorry I am. I never meant to hurt either of you. I had so much going on and—"

"It's okay, Caro. I was as much to blame as you. I immediately jumped to conclusions, out with the old, in with the new. That sort of thing. Howard and I struggle every day with losing Mark. I panicked when I thought I was losing you guys too. Let's forget about it and move on, shall we?"

"Yes, please. I love you, Fran."

"I love you, too, my sweet girl."

My heart soared as some of the burden was lifted from my weary soul. I'd fixed one thing going wrong in my life, now if I could figure out what to do about the rest...

We talked for a while about the new dog, Hailey's pony lessons, and my classes. I avoided the subject of Easton. Gratefully, Fran didn't bring him up either. When we finally ended the call, we both made a promise to speak tomorrow so Fran and Howard could talk to the kids.

After I ended the call, I realized Junie was sitting in the recliner. I hadn't noticed when she'd come into the room.

"Fran?" she asked.

"Yes, everything is good."

"I'm relieved."

"Am I being unreasonable, Junie?" I asked, bringing up a subject that had been on my mind for a few weeks.

"About what?" She glanced up from her phone. She'd been secretively texting someone quite a bit lately. As much as I wanted to pry, I didn't.

"Easton wanting to adopt Heath and Hailey."

Junie blinked a few times and squinted at me. She'd expected more conversation about Fran and Howard, and I'd done an end run on her. "You're being emotional, but changing your kids' last name and him legally adopting them is an emotional thing. It's permanent."

"But am I wrong?"

"I don't see it as right or wrong. Mark was in those kids' lives for six years. Easton will be in their lives for the rest of his life. That's a lot more than six years."

"You think I should let him change their last name?"

"I think you should think long and hard about the decision. Did you talk to Fran and Howard about it?"

"Oh, God, no. Not when I'm finally in their good graces again."

"You might want to see what they have to say about it," Junie suggested.

"Mark wouldn't have wanted it changed. It'd be like wiping out the last piece left of him."

"No, it wouldn't be. They'd still have their memories, and I know you. You'll make sure they remember him."

"If I changed it, then I wouldn't have the same last name as them."

"Is this about Mark or you?" Junie stared pointedly at me, and she might have hit the nail on the head. Was I being selfish and using Mark as an excuse?

"I don't trust Easton. What if he's trying to steal my children from me?"

"Are you listening to yourself?" Junie rolled her eyes and snorted. "Are you serious? I know he's not, and I don't know him nearly as well as you do. He's a good person, Caro. Why would he do something so damaging to you and the kids?"

Again, she was right, and I knew it. "I do miss him."

"I know you do."

"These past few weeks without him have been hell, but I've hurt him, too."

"Tell him you're sorry."

"I don't know where to start," I sighed.

"I know where you can start." She beamed as if she were the brightest best friend in the world.

"And where would that be?"

"Join him at the family skate."

"I don't know if I should," I hedged.

"I think you should."

"I don't know where my skates are."

"You're too organized not to know where they are."

Junie shot down every argument I had. She was right. I did know where my skates were. I also knew in my heart where I wanted to be and who I wanted to be doing it with.

I didn't know if the four of us would ever be a family, but I had to try, not just for the kids but for Easton and me. I owed myself that much. Mark was gone, and he wasn't coming back. This was my life now, and I had to stop living for someone who wasn't here anymore. My guilt over what happened was misplaced. I'd been a good wife, and he'd been a good husband. We hadn't been in love, and looking back, I don't know if we would've lasted over the long haul.

Easton and I had something special. We always had.

I needed to give us a chance.

--Easton--

My new year was starting out crappy.

On New Year's Eve, I'd joined the Puck Brothers, but no amount of alcohol dulled the pain inside me. I still had my kids, but I didn't have Caro. I didn't realize until that very moment how much that hurt. She didn't feel the same. She didn't trust me. She assumed the worst of me. She should know me better than that, but obviously we hadn't come very far since we'd reunited.

I insisted on time with the kids, and rather than being subjected to my company, she conceded by allowing me to take them on my own.

We had fun together, yet I missed her. I guess I'd harbored hope we'd form a family together.

Now I was at the family skate at the practice facility on the third Saturday in January with the twins. We sat on a row of bleachers while I laced up Hailey's figure skates, making sure they were tight enough to offer proper support. Heath insisted on doing his own, but I checked them afterward and did some minor adjustments. He was wide-eyed as he watched the skaters on the ice. Several of my teammates skated by with their kids. Even guys without kids were there, enjoying skating for the pure joy of it. All of us lived to skate, or we wouldn't be hockey players.

This was my first somewhat public outing with my kids, and I had cautioned my teammates not to mention I was their father. I hoped everyone remembered, but if they didn't, I'd deal with the fallout if I had to.

Straightening, I stood and reached for their hands. Hailey took mine and rose to her feet. She was fucking adorable in the pink skating outfit she'd insisted on wearing. Heath, on the other hand, wore the jersey I'd previously bought him. My heart swelled with pride seeing him in it, just as it had that first time I'd laid eyes on him. They were mine, and I was their dad. I would always be their protector, their port in a storm, and the guy who had their back.

"Why doesn't Mommy ever go with us?" Hailey asked me.

"Mom likes to skate," Heath added. I might be imagining things, but I thought I heard a note of accusation in his voice.

"I know. She's busy with school and all, but, yeah, she's a good skater." I put my arm around both their shoulders and guided them onto the ice.

"You've seen her skate?" Heath narrowed his eyes and studied me closely.

"I, uh, yeah, long time ago. I've known her since high school."

Heath was appeased by my answer and I blew out a relieved breath.

"I wish she was here." Hailey pouted and stomped her blades on the ice. I tamped down my panic. I wasn't sure how to diffuse Hailey if she went into full tantrum mode.

I didn't respond but began to skate with smooth, easy strokes of my blades on the ice. Heath pulled away as a couple other little boys raced by and gave chase. Hailey, usually outgoing, hung back.

"What's wrong, honey?"

"Daddy used to skate with us." She sniffled and looked away from me, staring into the distance at something I couldn't see. My heart constricted, not only because of the depth of her loss, but also for more selfish reasons. Would they ever call me Daddy? I didn't want to erase their memories of Mark but for them to create new memories with me. This was so hard, not knowing if I was doing or saying the right thing.

"I'm so sorry. I know it hurts." My words were lame, but what else did a guy say under these circumstances? I glanced around for a distraction and spotted our goalie Brick's little girl practicing spins at center ice. "Would you like to join Macy?" I pointed toward the pretty little girl who was Brick's pride and joy.

Hailey nodded, and I skated out to center ice with her. I introduced her to Macy and the two of them hit it off immediately. Before I knew it, I was left alone while my kids were skating all over the place.

"They're damn good on those blades," Ice said in my ear. I hadn't heard him skate up to me.

"Yeah, they are."

Someone had broken out the hockey sticks, and my son had grabbed one. He was big for his age and held his own with the older boys as they scrambled up and down the ice in an impromptu game. You couldn't get a bunch of hockey players together on the ice without someone finding sticks and a puck. Obviously, the same was true of our children.

"You're a lucky guy. Where's Caro?" He clapped me on the back and grinned at me. His own pregnant wife sat in the stands talking with some of the other WAGs.

"She didn't want to come. We're not on the best of terms." I met his gaze, and I wasn't fooling him.

"She'll come around, E. Or you can nudge her a little. Never hurts to say you're sorry. It might damage your pride a bit, but it's worth it."

"I don't know what I'd be sorry for. She doesn't trust me. She said so."

"Did you do something to cause her to mistrust you?"

I didn't think I did, but maybe I had by not discussing my plans with her. Instead I told her what I wanted. Maybe I did owe her an apology.

Ice coughed and inclined his head in the direction of the tunnel from the locker room to the ice. "Looks like someone changed their mind."

My head snapped in the direction he was looking. Before I'd even spotted her, my body knew she was here.

Caro stepped onto the ice, dressed in black tights and my jersey. Her blonde hair was pulled back in a sassy ponytail. Fuck, but she was stunning. My heart caught in my throat. By wearing my jersey, she was announcing to everyone in this place she was here for me and no one else. I skated toward her with strong, deliberate strokes of my blades, my eyes never straying from her beautiful face. She smiled tentatively, and I grinned like a damn fool. She met me halfway, and we stopped a few feet from each other, unmindful of the skaters skirting around us or the puck whizzing past us.

"You came." I stated the obvious and looked even more the fool, but I didn't care.

She nodded and reached for my hand. Together, we skated along the boards, trying to avoid the rambunctious hockey game going on around us. I only dared imagine what had brought her here. She'd dropped into my lap like my own personal angel from heaven.

"We're taking our lives in our hands," she said as a group of young boys chased down the puck a few feet from us with Heath in the lead.

"Watch me, Mom!" he yelled as he raced by. Caro beamed at him, ever the proud mother.

"Be careful!" she shouted.

"Yeah, we are. I've always liked living life on the edge." I smiled down at her, and her returning smile lit up my day.

"He's your son." She pointed toward Heath fighting for the puck with a bigger kid. Heath emerged victorious, took the puck several feet down the ice, and passed to a teammate.

"He is," I said proudly, as my chest puffed out a little. "And she's your daughter." I indicated Hailey, who was trading off spins with Macy.

"She's a scrapper like you though."

"And a neat freak like you."

"In some things. You saw her unwrap her present." She laughed, her eyes sparkling with good humor and something else I didn't dare name for fear I'd be wrong, but that something was there in her eyes. It gave me hope.

"Unwrap? She tore into it like a wild woman." We grinned at each other, and hope rose inside me. We could make this work.

"I think it's time we tell them," she said.

I stopped and spun to face her. I searched her face for any sign of teasing, but she was dead serious. "So do I. I think it's time for a lot of things."

"Like what?"

"I think we should try being a family." I held my breath and waited for her response.

"I'd like that." She placed her hands on my shoulders, leaned forward, and kissed me on the cheek. I broke into a wide grin.

"I love you, Caro. I never stopped loving you." The words came from deeper than my heart, more like my soul, my very core, the very thing that gave living things life. I loved her. Maybe I'd always loved her. But this time I loved her as a man loved a woman, and I intended to show her how much.

"I love you, too, Easton." Her blue eyes shone with the light of a thousand stars, and she was brighter than every one of them.

"It's taken me a long time to figure out what I wanted. I don't think I really knew until just now. I don't want today, or even tomorrow or next week, I want forever."

"So do I."

I bent down and kissed her in front of everyone. I might have lost the bet as Puck Brother, and I didn't care one damn bit. My teammates catcalled all around me but I ignored them.

This was what I'd wanted for longer than I realized.

Chapter Twenty-Nine

GOOD MORNING

--Caroline--

*E*aston stayed the night, and we made love well into the morning. Now I lay cuddled next to him at dawn, our naked bodies entwined. I wanted to wake up like this every morning for the rest of my life, but one step at a time.

We still had some talking to do.

He stirred and opened his eyes and a slow smile spread across his face. "Good morning, beautiful."

"Good morning to you." He ran his hand down my back and rested it on my bare ass. I laid my head on his chest.

"We need to talk."

"Oh, God, I hate the sound of those words. You're not going to boot me again, are you? No regrets, remember?"

I sat up. This needed to be a face-to-face conversation.

"I'm sorry," I said, and by the shock on his face, I could've knocked him down with a feather.

"Sorry?"

"My behavior. I've been really unfair to you. All you asked for was to be a part of our children's lives, and I fought you at every turn."

Easton nodded slowly, as if he were considering something. "I'm sorry, too, for pushing you when you weren't ready to be pushed, for not understanding what you're going through along with the kids. I'm not usually so impatient."

"I want to tell them, and I want them to have your last name."

"You do?" He blinked several times, then swiped his arm across his face. His eyes were suspiciously bright. "When should we tell them?"

"How about this morning?"

"This morning?" Now that the final moment of truth was upon him, he looked scared. "What if they throw a fit and hate the idea of me as their father? What if they blame you for keeping this secret from them?"

"They probably will, but we'll deal with it. Their anger or hurt won't last forever. They'll forgive us. You're a great father, and any child would be lucky to have you in their life."

"I could say the same about you. Let's do this."

I slid off the bed and held out my hand to him. He took a moment to survey my naked body with a naughty smile.

"What is it we're doing?" he joked, easing the tension slightly. I swatted at him. He caught my hand in his and kissed my knuckles.

I pulled away. "No more good stuff until we're done with the not-so-good stuff."

He sighed and stood, stretching his magnificent body and reaching for his clothes.

We showered and dressed. As hard as it was not to linger in the shower, we didn't. We had a mission, and we were both committed to our mission.

The kids didn't bat an eye when Easton and I walked out of the bedroom that morning. I'm not sure they understood what was going on, but they seemed okay with it. Junie was making breakfast, and the smell of bacon made my stomach growl.

After breakfast, we sat the kids down at the dining room table. Junie, guessing something big was going on, made herself scarce.

Heath sipped his juice and studied us with a solemn face, too serious for a kid his age. Hailey jabbered away, talking about her riding lessons, the pony she rode, her figure-skating routine, and a kid in her daycare she didn't like.

I held up a hand and smiled gently at her. "Hailey, honey, I need to you to be quiet and listen for a moment. Easton and I have something very important to tell you."

Hailey stopped in mid-sentence, her mouth forming a big *O*. She clasped her hands on the table in front of her and nodded, also serious for once.

I met Easton's gaze, and he squeezed my hand under the table. Turning back to my babies, I drew a deep breath and dived in. "There's no easy way to tell you this. Your dad, Mark, was a really good dad, and I never want to take that away from you, but the truth is that you have another dad." I paused, trying to find the words that six-year-olds would understand and coming up short. Both children stared at me with twin expressions of confusion.

"Like Julie at school has two dads? One is her stepdad, whatever that means," Hailey asked.

"No, not exactly. Easton is your father, your biological father. Mark was my husband and was also your father because of love, but not physically." I didn't know if what I was saying was over their heads or not.

"If Easton is our real father, why didn't we know until now?" Heath scowled and his eyes narrowed as he glared at me. My son was not happy.

Oh, God, this was difficult. "Easton and I knew each other years ago. I thought Mark was your biological father, but after he died, we did tests, and I found out Easton was."

Hailey's lip was quivering, and Heath's face was frozen solid with belligerence. I was making a huge mess of this. My news wasn't going over well at all. I looked to Easton for help.

"Hailey, Heath, I'm sorry I wasn't in your life earlier. Don't blame your mother. She simply didn't know. And you had a great dad. Now I'm here not to fill his shoes but to be a different kind of dad, the kind only I know how to be."

Hailey shook her head so hard her blonde curls slapped against her face. "No. No. No! You're not my daddy. My daddy is gone. I want him back. I want everything back the way it was. I hate this place. I hate you both. I want Nana and Grandpa. I want to go home." Hailey wailed with the pure emotions of a child, the pain so obvious I felt it in my heart and deep to my soul. Tears flowed down her face and huge sobs racked her small body. Heath threw his arms around her and glared accusingly at us over his shoulder. Hailey jerked away from him and ran down the hall to her bedroom.

Heath started after her and stopped. His eyes narrowed. "I want to go home too. Let us go home and live with Nana and Grandpa. We don't want to be here." He sprinted down the hallway and slammed his bedroom door.

For a long moment, Easton and I were silent, then our eyes met.

"That went well," Easton quipped. I wasn't in mood for levity and merely scowled at him.

"I need to talk to them." I started to get up, but Easton held me back with a gentle but firm hand on my arm.

"Give them time to absorb everything. This is lot for them to process."

"But I—"

He shook his head to silence me. "Give them a little time, honey. They're hurting, and I agree we shouldn't leave them alone too long."

"I shouldn't have told them yet. It's too soon. And you and I, they aren't going to like us together and we're—"

"You're not going to run on me again, are you?" Easton's brown eyes narrowed as he watched me intently.

"Run on you?"

"Kick me out. Tell we can't see each other. We're in this together, Caro. We agreed on that. You don't have to go through this alone."

"No, not this time," I admitted.

"We'll weather this storm together because that's how a family does it." He smiled, not one of his huge light-up-your-world smiles, because the situation didn't call for it, but a better-things-are-coming and a trust-in-me smile.

Tears slid down my cheeks, and he pulled me into his arms. I needed him, and that was okay. I'd tried so hard since Mark had died to be everything to everyone and to be independent, I found it hard to admit maybe I did need someone. That together we were stronger than we were apart.

Easton was the other half of me, and we would weather this storm.

--Easton--

There was no real handbook on parenting. Yeah, there were lots of books written on the subject, but I was beginning to discover that being a good parent relied more on instincts, love, fairness, and consistency.

I didn't have the solution on how to handle this sticky situation, but I decided that as long as we did it with love and the children's best interests at heart, eventually things would work out.

We'd dropped a bombshell on them, and they would need time to adjust, but kids were resilient and sometimes they handled changes better than adults did.

We gave them about a half hour to let their emotions out. I don't know if that was the right thing to do or not, but approaching them immediately seemed counterproductive to me, and Caro agreed.

"I'll talk to Heath if you want to tackle Hailey?" I said.

Caro nodded, her face blotchy from crying. She blew her nose, wiped her face, and gave me a shaky smile. "We can do this."

I stood and pulled her to her feet. I gave her a soft kiss on the lips and winked. "We *can* do this. Divide and conquer."

She almost laughed. Together, we walked down the hall and knocked on the kids' bedroom doors.

Neither of them said a word, so with one last encouraging smile in Caro's direction, I went inside as did she.

Heath was sitting on his bed tossing a puck back and forth from one hand to the other. "Ziggy, one of my teammates, can juggle six pucks at once."

My son didn't look up, just kept doing what he was doing.

"One time he tried seven and got smacked in the head with multiple pucks, almost knocked him out." I chuckled and waited for a reaction. Nothing happened. The room was silent except for the slapping sound the puck made as it hit his palm.

Smack. Smack. Smack.

"I know you're upset and have every right to be. It's not easy to find out things aren't as you always thought they were."

Smack. Smack. Smack.

"I know you loved your dad, and I never want to take that away from you. I'm just hoping that someday, you'll find room in your heart for me too. I want to be your dad, Heath. I want to cheer you on at your hockey games. I want to help you with your homework. I want to teach you to drive a car. I want to be there for you when you need me for the rest of my life."

Smack. Smack. Thump.

The two pucks hit the ground, and Heath didn't bother to pick them up. He lifted his head and our gazes met. His eyes were filled with unshed tears, and my heart broke a little.

"I miss my dad."

"I know you do, buddy. It'll get easier, and you'll always have the memories." I sat on the edge of the bed, keeping a foot between us, not wanting to push it by getting too close. "I know how it feels to lose a dad. I lost mine. I'll never forget the night they came to our door to tell my mom. It's burned in my memory, but as time goes on, the good memories are the ones I choose to recall and hold close to my heart."

"How did you lose your dad?" He sniffled.

"He was a firefighter. He died trying to save someone. He was a hero."

"My dad didn't die trying to save someone."

"That's okay. He's still your hero, right?"

Heath nodded. "I guess so." He scooted over, closing the foot between us, and wrapped his arms around my waist. I hugged him close and let him cry, possibly for the first time since his father had died.

--Caroline--

Because of my controlling nature and tendency to believe no one else could possibly know what to do in this situation better than me, my first inclination was to insist that I talk to both children. Mark had let me do all the hard parenting, while he'd been the fun parent. The fact that Easton wanted to help with the good and bad stuff was something I should encourage, not discourage, so I curbed my initial reaction and agreed to let Easton talk with Heath while I spoke with Hailey.

I opened the door. She was facedown, her head buried in her pillow, and her arms wrapped around the teddy bear Mark had bought her last Christmas.

I sat down on the bed and put my hand on her back. She jerked away. She was going to be a tough cookie. She'd been Daddy's girl and had also been overly attached to her grandmother.

"I know you miss him, honey. I know this is hard. Easton doesn't want to replace your dad. He just wants to be part of your life. He loves you too. It's okay to like him. You're not being disloyal. Your dad would want you to be happy first and foremost."

Hailey shook her head and kicked her feet.

I sighed, wishing I had all the clever answers, but right now I was floundering. Hailey was crying again, her body shaking once more with sobs. I placed a hand on her back, and this time she didn't pull away. I stroked her back and sang one of her favorite songs, "When You Wish Upon a Star." Eventually, she was quiet, and I thought she'd fallen asleep.

She surprised me when she sat up and rubbed her eyes. She gazed up at me and blinked several times. Her expression was one of fear and sadness, but not anger.

"Oh, honey." I pulled her into my arms and held her tightly. She hugged me back, still sniffling. "It's all going to be okay. You have lots of people who love you."

"I know."

I stroked her hair and held her against me. She hugged me tight.

A few minutes later, we walked into the living room, hand in hand. Easton and Heath were completely immersed in a video game. Easton glanced up briefly and winked at me. I winked back.

I knew right then everything was going to be okay.

Chapter Thirty

ROUTINES

--Caroline--

By mid-February, we were settling into a routine. Easton pretty much lived in our condo, and I wasn't about to complain.

The twins still had their moments, but their attitudes were slowly improving, and they'd warmed up to Easton even more than before. They didn't call him Dad, but that'd come with time.

That Sunday, Easton proposed we take a drive to Cooper and Izzy's house. They lived in one of the older neighborhoods in Seattle where all the timber barons and shipping magnates had once lived. The houses were huge and well maintained despite their age, and many, like Cooper's, had incredible water views. I never tired of looking at them, even if only from the street.

We promised the kids ice cream when we finished. Even though the day was cold and dreary, they didn't care. They wanted their ice cream.

The four of us piled in his SUV with Mona in the back and drove up the hill. Easton turned down a street before Coop's.

"Hey, isn't this the wrong street?"

"I want to show you something." He was acting very suspicious, and I didn't have any idea what he might be up to. The kids were arguing in the back seat and not paying any attention.

He pulled down a long, winding driveway. The bushes and trees needed a good trimming. As the driveway opened up, there was an unkempt lawn and a large, craftsman-style mansion. It was in need of TLC and a good coat of paint, but the house was beautiful, with a wide front porch that wrapped around to the back.

"Want to see it? I happen to have a key."

"Why would you have a key to this house?"

"Just go along with me." He got out of the car and opened the passenger door. The kids piled out along with Mona and ran up the cracked and uneven sidewalk, overgrown with weeds, and onto the porch, peeking in the windows.

Easton took my hand. "A condo is no place to raise kids, and Mona needs room to run. Rusty needs mice to hunt. I know it needs work, but I thought you and I would have a good time fixing it up together. My realtor assures me it has good bones, and all the repairs are cosmetic."

I gaped at him in absolute shock. "What are you saying?"

"It's ours." He pushed open the door as he said the words, and the kids ran shouting happily into the house.

I walked inside the old house and stared in absolute wonder at the woodwork and the hardwood floors. We walked to the back and the view of Puget Sound was spectacular. The backyard was large, with ample space for kids and dog to run and play.

Heath emerged from one of the rooms and stopped in front of us. "Mom, you have to see this huge fireplace." He hesitated, his solemn dark eyes focused on me. "You need to see it, too, Dad."

My eyes filled with tears, and when I glanced at Easton, he was wiping his face. "We'll be right there." His husky voice cracked, and I smiled encouragingly at him.

"Mommy, Daddy, hurry. Come see this room," Hailey, not to be outdone by her brother, shouted at us.

A lone tear slid down Easton's face, and I kissed his cheek, tasting the saltiness.

"I've looked forward to the day they'd call me Dad."

"So have I." I winked at him and gazed around the house. "This place looks like a lot of work."

Easton frowned. "You don't like it?"

"I love it." I threw my arms around his neck and kissed him. "And I love you."

"I love you, too, baby."

We turned, arm in arm, and walked down the hall of our new home, as my mind filled with all kinds of possibilities. Yes, life was good. And life with Easton was even better.

This house was ours forever, and we'd restore it together with love and passion, just like we'd do everything.

Together. Forever.

EPILOGUE

--Easton--

"*Y*ou missed a spot, buddy." Kaden pointed at his gleaming black skate. With a growl, I bent over the skate again and buffed the leather. The damn thing was so well polished it was blinding me.

"You're next, asshole," I warned him. "You're pretty much tied at the hip to your mystery woman."

"Hey, hurry up, I don't have all day. You've spent the last half hour on his skates," Ziggy shouted from across the locker room.

"Get in line. I've been waiting longer," argued Steele.

"Fuck. You guys are pissing me off." I stood, grabbed my supplies, and walked over to Kaden's boots. I swear the asshole had soaked them in mud before I got here.

"You gotta pay the price for losing the Puck Brothers bet." Ziggy grinned.

"Look at the bright side. You only have to polish our boots until the end of the hockey season," Cave pointed out.

"And that's the bright side? What the fuck, Kaden, did something crawl in your boots and die in there? They fucking stink." I was cranky, but I tried to tell myself it could be worse. They could've made me dance on drag queen night at the Westside Pub, which was one of their options they'd voted on.

"Get to work. I don't have all day." Kaden grinned down at me and cracked an invisible whip.

I flipped him off. "Fuck you, asshole."

"Someone is a sore loser," Ziggy laughed.

"Yeah, just wait, assholes, your day will come."

"Never," they said in unison, and I knew they were dead wrong, but I couldn't tell them that any more than someone could've told me all those months ago.

Love isn't something you can plan for. It hits you over the head when you're least expecting it, and no matter how strong your defenses, the right woman finds a way through to your heart.

- THE END -

Thank you for spending time in my world. I hope you enjoyed reading this book. If you did, please help other readers discover this book by leaving a review.

For news on upcoming Jami Davenport books, **sign up for my newsletter by clicking here**.

Did you find any errors? Please email me so I may correct them and upload a new version. You can reach me via the contact page on my website: https://www.jamidavenport.com/contact/

COMPLETE BOOKLIST

The following Jami Davenport titles are available in digital and many are available as trade paperbacks. These books can be read as standalones.

Scoring Series

Introducing the Puck Brothers

Shutout

Blocked

Playmaker

Icing

Faceoff (May 2021)

Moo U (World of True North)

Gametime (April 2021)

Seattle Sockeyes Hockey

Skating on Thin Ice

Crashing the Net

Love at First Snow

Melting Ice

Hearts on Ice

Bodychecking

Goaltending

Penalty Play

Shutdown Player

Shot on Goal

Deflected

Seattle Skookums Baseball

Bottom of the Ninth

Men of Tyee
Sacked in Seattle
Tackled in Seattle

Seattle Steelheads
Kickoff (The Originals)
Snap Decision (The Originals)
Offsides (The Originals)
Draw Play (The Originals)
Hot Read (The Originals)
Comeback Route (The Originals)
Blindsided
Game Changer
Fumble Recovery

Gone Missing Investigations
Gone Missing

Evergreen Nights Series
Save the Last Dance
Who's Been Sleeping in My Bed?
The Gift Horse

Standalone Books
Madrona Sunset

ABOUT THE AUTHOR

Subscribe to my newsletter to receive free digital books and be notified of new releases, special sales, and contests: https://eepurl.com/LpfaL

USA Today bestselling author Jami Davenport writes sexy contemporary, new adult, and sports romances, and has recently dived into Romantic Suspense with her new series, *Gone Missing*.

Jami lives on a small farm in the woods near Puget Sound with her Green Beret-turned-plumber husband, a Newfoundland drool monster, and a prince disguised as an orange tabby cat.

Jami worked in IT for years and is a former high school business teacher but recently achieved her life-long dream and is now a full-time author. A horse lover since birth, Jami showed dressage horses for over thirty years. Now she gardens and goes RVing in her green Winnebago Minnie, along with other travelling adventures. She's a lifetime Seahawks and Mariners fan and is impatiently waiting for the day professional hockey comes to Seattle. Jami still misses her SuperSonics. An avid boater, Jami has spent countless hours in the San Juan Islands, a common setting in her books. In her opinion, it's the most beautiful place on earth.

Website: https://www.jamidavenport.com

Join my reader group:
https://www.facebook.com/groups/BleachersandBooks/

facebook.com/jamidavenportauthor
twitter.com/jamidavenport
instagram.com/jamidavenportauthor
bookbub.com/authors/jami-davenport